AIDA TIME

STITCHES IN CRIME
BOOK 10

ACF BOOKENS

1

I have a knack for two things—starting projects at the worst possible time *and* starting too many projects at once. Fortunately, my second problem wasn't as much of a problem right now because the shop was well-staffed by Claire, and I didn't have to do any salvaging or run the store for the rest of the week.

The first problem, though? Now that was a big one because it was approximately 853 degrees outside, and if it were more humid, I would be swimming. This was definitely not the ideal time of year to start a renovation project in Virginia.

But I wanted to finish this project before our friends from out of town arrived in two weeks so that they could crash on cots in the space without roasting to death. Plus, I wanted the room for my at-home office when it wasn't being used as a guestroom.

The summer kitchen had been standing since my old farmhouse was built about 1850 and was in great shape. In fact, you could still see the soot marks on the ceiling from where the stove had been, and the floorboards were mostly intact. All in all, the bulk of the work was going to be on making the space comfortable. I couldn't imagine being a likely enslaved woman working in this space. It must have been so very hot.

Now, with Sawyer off at preschool and a full five hours of open time ahead of me, I was ready to begin. I stood outside the ten-by-twelve building and smiled. She was already a beauty, and I was so excited to turn her into more than a storage spot. And that was where I was going to begin—hauling out all the stuff.

I began with the old makeshift shelves that the previous owners had installed. They were made of reused plywood and strips of leftover lumber and came down easily with a few whacks of the crowbar. Then I hauled the leftover baseboards and crown molding off the rafters where they had been stored and stacked them by the driveway to take to the shop later. Finally, I removed a few totes of holiday decorations I had stored in there and decided I'd have to make part of the rafters a storage loft since my small house had no space for these things. For now, though, they were waterproof enough to sit under the eaves for a few days.

I was already soaked through when I heard a car pull up, and I walked around the house to see my fiancé, Santiago, standing next to his car in torn jeans and a T-shirt.

"I'm ready to work," he said.

I laughed. "I thought you were on duty today?" Santi was the sheriff in town, and given that we only had a few police officers, he wasn't often able to get a day off.

"Watson is covering," he said, "and that new deputy from over in Albemarle is great. Didn't need much training at all, so the two of them have it covered." He leaned over and kissed my cheek. "Now, I'm here to help us get our new office ready."

Santi moved in with me a few months back and has been all about the projects ever since. Our yard was now landscaped beautifully, and all the walls that Sawyer had "decorated" with markers were repainted, except for Santi's closet, which he insisted on keeping as-is. He loved the whimsical scribbles of his soon-to-be stepson. We even had a new permanent island in the kitchen. The house was in good shape.

This project was next on the list, and I was not going to turn down Santi's help, especially since the labor was going to be extensive. "Okay, then, first things first. We need to contend with that back corner where the floor rotted through." It looked like the old chimney had leaked at some point, and the previous owners had patched the rotting floor with a piece of thick plywood. It was a great fix for a storage shed but not so great for a guest or office space.

We walked to the back corner, and I immediately decided we needed lights. Now, I could have rented those construction lights that would have lit up the space like a movie shoot, but that would have required me to think ahead. Instead, I duct-taped my flashlight to the rafter, and we set to work.

A lot of grunting later, we had the plywood up, and it was clear that a lot of the floor in this part of the building would need to be replaced. "So, I have some boards at the shop we can use. They won't be an exact match, but it'll be close enough," I said.

"Alrighty then. I saw your dad's truck out front. You borrowing it?" Santi asked.

"Yep, just for today so we can haul what we need. I figured we could drop off the stuff out front and pick up the boards. Maybe do a quick run to the hardware store for insulation and Sheetrock?"

"Sounds perfect," he said, "as long as we get to go to Murphy's for their maple bacon bagel."

"Of course. What would a workday be without bacon, maple-pistachio cream cheese, and a cinnamon bagel." This place had the best bagels, and we tried to go there as often as our budget allowed. "Plus, I think I'm due a free latte on my punch card."

"Bonus," Santi said as he helped me load the boards into the truck before we headed up the road to my shop and my friend Saul's construction yard. It was prime building season for his team, so when we pulled in, the place was pretty empty except for Claire's car and one other in the lot by the shop.

"Let's just stack this over there," I said, pointing to the lean-top at the edge of the house that now housed my shop. The two of us unloaded all the wood and then stood back, admiring our work. "Well, that's probably enough for the day?" I joked.

"Absolutely," Santi said as he stretched. "But maybe we should, you know, check in with Claire to be sure she doesn't need anything. Keep up appearances as business owners."

I laughed. "Fair enough." We wandered into my shop and found Claire at the register, tagging more crystal doorknobs from our back stock. These were consistently my bestseller, and now, my friends and family were looking for them at yard sales and even in people's junk drawers. We sold a lot just as door-knobs, but Claire had also begun to create some amazing coat hangers and these abstract pieces of reclaimed wood and mandala-like shapes from the knobs. They were gorgeous, and I planned to buy one from myself for our house soon.

"Busy morning?" I asked my clerk as she looked up and smiled.

"Steady. Got a call about these." She tapped a couple of doorknobs with her long nail. "So I wanted to be sure we had plenty ready."

"Nice. If you hear of someone with a secret stash of knobs in their attic—"

"I know who to call," she said. "Got prices in mind for what you just brought?"

"Nah. Most of it's pretty contemporary stuff, so sell it by the piece or the lot for whatever you think." Anything I'd make on those items was profit, after all.

"Got it," Claire said as she resumed pricing. "Anything else you need me to focus on today?"

"Nah, I just wanted to check in," I said with a glance toward Santi. "He said it's what I'm supposed to do as a business owner."

"You're the owner?" a man said from the stairwell to my left.

After I calmed my heartrate from the startle, I smiled and put out my hand. "Sure am. Paisley Sutton. Can I help you with something?"

The big, bear-like man shook my hand. "Horatio Denver," he said. "I'm an architect, and I hear you have some of the best salvage in the Blue Ridge."

I blushed. "At the risk of sounding arrogant, I can't say I disagree. Were you looking for anything in particular?"

"Big stuff, actually," he said. "Mantels. Doorframes. Stained glass windows."

This was the kind of customer I loved most. They knew what they wanted and what was reasonable to pay, and while they might haggle a bit, they were mostly willing to pay what I asked. Plus, I got to clear some floor space.

Santi laughed. "Oh boy, you're in for a treat, sir."

Horatio smiled. "Thanks, Sheriff."

"He's not wrong," I said with a grin at my fiancé. "We have a large selection of those things out under the barn. Claire can show you around, and we can have anything you need to be delivered later in the week, free of charge."

"Hot dog," he said. "Mind if I ask? Do you have any really big stained glass pieces? Like six feet by three feet or so?"

This sale was getting better and better. "We just salvaged an entire church's worth." I turned to Claire. "You know where we put those, right?"

"Back of the barn in the sliders?" she asked.

"Exactly," I said as I held out my hand to Horatio again. "You're in good hands with Claire, but don't hesitate to email me if you have any specific questions or need anything special. Sometimes I can rustle up requests." I handed him my card and waved as Santiago and I headed back to the truck.

"Cha-ching," Santi said as he got into the truck's passenger side. "That should be a great payday."

I nodded. "Especially if he takes some of that stained glass. They're beautiful pieces but huge and not the right fit for everyone's home." I started the truck and got us back on the road. "I had thought a new church might want them or maybe a bar or something, but if he wants to buy one for a house, by all means."

"I have a hard time picturing good ole St. Peter in the living room myself, but to each his own," Santi said with a laugh.

I knew what he meant. I loved the pieces myself, especially since they were done in such vibrant colors. And my friend Wayne Cain, who was a master stained glass craftsman down below Charlottesville, had said they were well-made and in good shape. But I just couldn't picture them in our old farmhouse.

WHEN WE PULLED up to the farmhouse, I glanced at the thermometer hanging on the porch—ninety-two in the shade, and the office was in full sun. It was going to be a hot day, and that called for the southern solution to humid heat—sweet tea. Fortunately, I'd brewed a batch the night before, so I poured Santi and myself big glasses full and followed him back outside.

I stared at the back of the building for a moment as I took a long sip of my tea, and then I finally said, "I guess I've put this off long enough."

"Here we go, huh?" Santi said as he picked up the crowbar. "You want to do the honors?"

"Sure," I said and put down my glass. The floorboards were so weak that they came out as more powder than wood, and by the time I'd gotten through three pieces, I knew we were going to have to take up most of the floor. "Termites!" I shouted over and over as I jerked up fragments of the flooring.

Finally, probably fearing for his own safety, Santi took the crowbar from me and said, "Alright there, GI Jane. Let me take over for a while."

I rolled my eyes and headed over to my glass, which Santi had thoughtfully covered with a fragment of Sheetrock to protect it from the insect-made dust in the air. I pulled long and hard on the glass as I watched Santi test each board and then pull it up as he made his way toward me and the front of the office.

He was about halfway across the small room when the crowbar went right through the board, as it had been doing, but this time, it made a cracking sound as it reached the ground. Instinctively, I winced. Nothing ever good came from that sound.

As I walked over, Santi peered below the partially removed board, shook his head, and then pulled up the rest of it. He then looked up at me, said, "I'm so sorry," and pulled up another three feet of boards in front of him, even though many of them seemed intact.

With a lot of will, I forced myself to watch without bemoaning the loss of all that beautiful hardwood that was splintering with every tug of Santi's arms. But I knew my fiancé would not destroy more than what was necessary, and I guess, somewhere deep down, I probably knew why he was ripping up even more of the floor.

Sure enough, when he stopped feverishly removing the boards and stood back as the dust settled, there it was, a human skeleton right below where I had planned to place my clerk's desk.

I threw back my head and moaned.

2

At some point, a person has to consider that they might be the cause of their own strife. I was that person at that moment. This was the tenth body I'd found, and I was seriously concerned about what energy I had put into the universe if the universe kept sending me bodies.

Perhaps the only thing that kept me from totally sinking into a well of self-pity and despair was that my fiancé, the county sheriff, never implied any such thing. In fact, he seemed to think it a sort of boon that I was helping to bring answers and sometimes healing to the families and friends of these victims. I was in two minds about that.

On the one hand, I was glad we were discovering these bodies and solving their murders, but on the other, I was ready to pass the baton and let someone else continue the race for justice.

Today, though, I was in the thick of it, and Santi and I had to do some quick work to manage the situation. First, I called my dad and asked him to pick up Sawyer from school. I didn't need a busy preschooler coming in with his little shovel to help dig up bones. He was currently big into dinosaurs, and I could just see him thinking he was on a dig for the latest T. rex skeleton.

Meanwhile, Santi now had to deal with a crime scene, so he called Savannah Watson, his head deputy, and then gave our friend Alex, the coroner, a ring.

With all our calls made and our people squared, Santi and I moved to the edge of the office door and sat down. We couldn't do anything more on the office or the skeleton until Santi and his team cleared the scene, and I knew that would be a long afternoon and evening of work.

I put my head against his shoulder and moaned again. "I really just wanted to get my office ready."

He kissed the crown of my head and said, "I know, Pais. I know. We'll take care of this situation ASAP, and we still have the rest of the week to finish the office."

I sat up and looked at him. "The rest of the week?"

"Yep, I was going to surprise you each morning, but I think it might be helpful for you to know now that I took the entire week off to do this project with you." A small crease formed between his eyebrows. "Is that okay?"

"Okay?" I said. "That's more than okay. That's amazing. Thank you." I kissed him on the cheek, aware that someone's remains lay in the dirt behind us. "And that news makes me determined to see some hope in this situation." I stood and stretched as I looked back toward the poor person tucked under my office.

"Like what?" Santi said as he rose from the floor and put his arm on my shoulders.

"Well, first, Sawyer didn't find the body." Just the idea of it made me shudder. That boy had brought me dog poop in a pizza box, the skin of a deer, and any number of partially maimed worms. It would not be a stretch for him to carry a human femur into the living room to show me.

"That's a big one," Santi said. "What else?"

"As you always say, this is the chance to find answers and hopefully help someone who has a lot of questions."

He nodded. "Two very good things."

I felt a little mischievous, so I said, "And finally, I get to solve another murder."

At this, the sheriff rolled his eyes. "Really?"

"I have the week off, and I hear the sheriff is off this week, too. So I have the time, and there appears to be a need." I grinned at him.

"I'm not even going to dignify that with a response," he said as he headed toward the sound of tires on my gravel driveway. Someone was already here.

When we came around the house, Savannah was standing in the driveway with her hands folded in front of her.

"You okay?" I said as I walked over and hugged her.

"Are *you* okay? You just found a body at your house, Paisley," she said.

I nodded. "It's a skeleton, so that helps. At least the person didn't die recently," I said. "But yeah, it's a lot."

"I'll say," she said. "Where are we working?"

Santi led her around the house while I slipped inside to get her a glass of tea and put another pitcher out in the sun to brew. The heat wasn't going to quit, and we couldn't either. Someone needed to be identified and accounted for, and none of us would stop until that happened.

BY THE TIME Alex had removed the body an hour or so later, we knew the victim was male, probably African American, and had been under my office for a very, very long time. Alex wasn't yet ready to speculate on how long "very, very" was, but I didn't have a good feeling about that projected time frame, given the history of my property.

. . .

THE HOUSE WAS BUILT SOMETIME in the mid-nineteenth century
—at least, that's the best I could tell from the shape of the nail
heads in my attic. Given that the land around us was still largely
rural, pastured, and very, very rich, I expected this farmstead
had been one that used enslaved laborers to assist with farm
chores.

My property would never have been a plantation in the
formal sense, given that it was small and probably required the
White owners to work alongside the Black people they
enslaved, yet I had always assumed people had been enslaved
here. We even had two depressions in the backyard that seemed
like they could be the remnants of where slave quarters had
once stood.

Short of a full-scale archaeological or archival investigation,
however, I hadn't thought I'd ever have evidence of that history.
Now, though, it seemed likely that the person we'd discovered
under the floor might have been an enslaved man, and the
possible ways this man could have ended up under the summer
kitchen at the place where he lived and worked gave me chills.

Still, I forced myself not to get too far into that thinking
until we had specific information about the man's identity and
how long ago he had died. Until we had that information, I
wasn't going to speculate. Instead, I was going to crawl on my
belly under my office and gather any materials from there that
might be useful in solving this murder.

"I'm going under for evidence," I said to Santi and
Savannah as I prepared to slither under the building.

"We don't know that there was a crime committed here,
Pais," Santi said.

I poked my head back out from under the building and
looked at my beautiful, very logic-focused fiancé. "Seriously?
You think someone crawled under the kitchen to die of natural

causes?" I shook my head and continued my snake-like wiggle further under the building.

Santi was great at his job because he didn't leap to conclusions, and I knew that he felt that this was murder as much as I did, but he wasn't going to say that until we had actual proof.

That proof came to light almost as soon as I got to where the skeleton had been when a piece of metal gouged into my leather glove as I pulled myself along the ground. Luckily, I felt the tug on the fabric before it went further. Otherwise, I would have had a bloody, dusty murder knife stuck in the fleshy part of my thumb. Instead, I pulled the knife free of my glove and passed it up through the hole above my head. "That's blood, right?"

Savannah took the long, thin knife and studied the dark brown substance on the blade. "Looks to be." She sighed and nodded at me. "It could be animal blood, though," she said.

I pursed my lips and nodded. "It *could* be, but I'm going to wager it isn't." I turned my body around in a circle but didn't see anything else under the building, not even trash. That was odd since a lot of people used to—and sometimes still did—use the undersides of their buildings as places to dump trash that didn't biodegrade. I couldn't tell you the number of buildings I'd taken down only to find a treasure trove of old bottles and cans underneath.

"I don't see anything else under here, so I'm heading back out." I backed out from under the building even as I wished it sat just a bit higher off the ground so I could simply get out through the hole in the floor. "And now, I need to do more work, or I need a shower," I said as I walked back through the office door and faced the two police officers.

"I'm going to get this back to the station and send a sample off to the lab. I'll put a rush on it." Savannah wiped a cloud of dust off my back as she passed me. "If I were you, I'd take that shower."

She didn't have to say it, but I knew what she meant. I had just crawled through someone's decomposed dust. Somehow, though, that didn't bother me, and I could feel the energy crawling under my skin. "I hear you on that, but honestly, I kind of want to do some more work."

Savannah shook her head and waved. "I'll let you know what we know when we know it." She then headed toward her car.

"Working sounds good to me, too," Santi said as he kissed my dusty cheek. "We aren't going to have those results or more information until at least tomorrow. And I don't think I can just sit around waiting."

"My thoughts exactly," I said as I picked up the crowbar. "Any more of this floor need to go?"

A FEW HOURS LATER, Santi and I had removed the last of the rotten floorboards, and we had begun feathering in the wide, plank boards we had brought home from my salvage supply. They were slightly thinner than the originals but, by and large, were the same size. And with some sanding and staining, everything would eventually match pretty well. I was pleased with how they looked.

But I was even more pleased that we had closed the hole before Sawyer arrived. The last thing I needed was my kid sticking himself or any other number of objects down into it. As he ran over, scattering our chickens with his excitement, I had a vision of a cache of eggs slowly rotting in the heat beneath the floor. I shuddered and then quickly realized that my imagination had brought up a big question—if someone's body had been tucked under the floor, how had no one noticed? After all, the decomposition process, be it eggs or humans, was not an odor-free one.

That question would have to wait, though, because I

desperately needed a shower, as did Santi, and given the fidgety grumpiness of a certain child, he needed dinner. I invited Dad to stay with us for the fascinating dinner of chicken nuggets and Tater Tots made in the air fryer, but he declined the delicacy, saying that Lucille, my stepmother, had dinner waiting for him at home.

"I'll be back tomorrow, though. Looks like you're ready to insulate and hang Sheetrock." My dad was past the point of having any business lifting sheets of heavy plasterboard into place, but I knew better than to say that. "Pick the supplies up on my way in?"

I tossed him the keys to his truck and said, "Sounds good."

"Your keys are in your car," he said. "See you in the morning." If I wasn't mistaken, there was a little jaunt in his step. My dad did love a project.

Santi grabbed a shower first while I asked Sawyer about his day and made dinner. My son was quite talkative when he wanted to be, but when he wasn't inclined, he had two standard answers to my usual questions—"What did you do at school today?" was often answered with "play" and "Anything special happen at school today?" elicited a "nope."

Apparently, he had had enough interaction and energy release today because he settled onto the couch with his Nintendo Switch and sent Sonic gathering rings across the universe. I was grateful for the space and alone time to just think. Today had been a lot to take in, and I wasn't one of those people who could fully process with others around, even if they were the people I loved best.

As I washed the filth from my hands and laid the gourmet, organic Taters Tots that Sawyer loved best on the air fryer tray with a mass of nuggets, I pondered the man who had been under my office all this time. I didn't get very far, though, since I didn't know anything about him. The edgy expectation of what

Alex would tell us tomorrow, hopefully, flowed under my skin like poison ivy. I hoped I could sleep.

It turned out that after a shower, some good fried food, and an episode of *Raising Dion*, I was half-asleep. So I climbed into bed after I put Sawyer down and slept for almost ten hours. Clearly, I was tired.

The next morning, though, I got Sawyer off to school, and then after recovering with a cup of coffee from the exertion it was to get a young child into clothing and fed, I was outside and ready to work. By then, Dad and Santi had been at it for a couple of hours, so I shouldn't have been surprised that all the insulation was already in and the Sheetrock was going up.

I was glad I made it out when I did because they were ready to put the first full sheet of plaster up on the ceiling, something my dad, with his degenerating disks in his neck, did not need to be doing. I stepped in and asked him to please guide us in placement and to drill in the first couple of screws.

With that system in place, the three of us had the ceiling Sheetrocked and the light fixture up in just a couple of hours. I had chosen a simple antique chandelier to hang in the space, which was a choice that surprised me because I hadn't always been interested in crystals and sparkles. Now, though, I loved the look of this simple wrought-iron piece. It didn't hang very low in the room and gave off a beautiful, gentle light that spread to all the corners.

"Lovely," I said when Santi flipped the switch and turned it on.

The three of us spent the rest of the morning hanging plasterboard and cutting bits out for the outlets I'd had the electrician install a few weeks before. I went a little overboard on the number of outlets, but after living in an old farmhouse and having no outlets in some rooms and only one in the bathroom, I was erring on the side of caution.

The electrician had also put in the mini-split-heating unit I was installing to keep the place comfortable, so we got that rocked in and took a break for lunch. I had a ton of sandwich makings available, so I set up a spread on the kitchen counter and let Dad and Santi serve themselves while I tended to my Maine Coon cat Beauregard's long list of requests, such as fresh water—despite the fact I had put some out just this morning—and the rearrangement of his afghan on the sofa. He could not possibly abide a wrinkle, now could he?

I let the grumpy guy sleep through lunch, but when we'd all finished our meal, I leashed him up and put him on the long lead I had running out by the garden so he could prance around and pretend to hunt a bit. He was a bit like a billionaire hiring someone to take him on safari with his pretty paws and his desire to stay completely out of the dirt, but I loved watching him leap at grasshoppers like a fierce if slightly ineffective lion.

The rest of the afternoon's work went well for most of us, but Beau grew weary of the discomfort of having to lay on the actual ground and serenaded us for the better part of an hour before I couldn't take his yowling anymore and put him inside —after smoothing his blanket, of course. We three humans clipped along at a great pace, and by the time I left to get Sawyer from school, the men were hanging the final piece of drywall.

While I was gone, the coroner, Alex, called, and after Dad took Sawyer to help him pick up the trim boards and paint, Santi caught me up. "Black male. Approximately thirty to fifty. Stabbed."

I nodded. "Okay, and does he have an age for the bones?" This was the part I was most interested in, after all.

Santi sighed. "Yeah, approximately 135-150 years old."

"So he might have been enslaved here, then." I'd done enough research of African American history to know that you couldn't assume all Black people in the US were enslaved during that period. Some were free people of color, but sadly, most had been subjected to that awful system. "The dates make it possible, at least."

"It does seem so," Santi said. "I'd say we could run dental records and such..."

"But it wouldn't do any good given the bones are that old and he was a Black man. No records." Tears sprang to my eyes. "I need to find out who he was, Santi."

He came over and put his arms around me. "I know, and we'll do our best." He squeezed me tighter and then let me go. "Why don't you go see Xzanthia? I'll clean up here and wait for your dad and Sawyer."

"Okay, cool. You don't mind me looking into this?" I had overstepped in the past and made Santi's job harder. I definitely didn't want to do that again.

"Not at all. I don't know that policework is going to solve this one, Pais, so you do your thing." He squeezed my arm. "Now go before that boy comes home and cons his mama into staying home."

Taking his words to heart, I jogged inside for my wallet and keys, then jumped into the car to head to town. The Octonia Historical Society was one of my favorite places, and Xzanthia Nicholas, the society's director, was one of my favorite people. She had done a lot of research into the communities of enslaved workers in our county, and I knew she'd be eager to help identify this man if that was possible.

But first, I needed coffee and a brief visit with my best friend, Mika, whose shop happened to be just up the street from the historical society. I had texted her last night to tell her about the skeleton, and she had just about as many questions as I had. I knew she'd be interested to learn what we knew now. I also knew she'd be eager to help with the research.

So with two huge decaf vanilla lattes in hand, I headed over to see Mika in her yarn store. As usual, she was arms deep in bins of yarn, this time being beautiful organic cotton that I wanted to dive into head first.

"I bring coffee and information," I said as she smiled at me when I came in.

"Ooh, I'm not sure which I'm more excited about," Mika said as she stacked baby-pink yarn on a small shelf by the door. "But of course, coffee first." She took the mug and led the way to her cozy corner, a secluded set of chairs and a table where people would knit or crochet and just relax. "Now, the news, please."

I told her about what Alex had found, and she whistled. "Well, that's a lot. So you think he was enslaved?"

"I expect so. I'm actually on my way to see Xzanthia to start some research." When my best friend lowered her head and looked out under her eyebrows, I quickly said, "With Santi's blessing. He doesn't think he can find much using modern methods."

She let out a long breath. "That makes sense, but you'll be careful, right? As we've learned, even long-ago deaths have a way of bringing out the worst in folks."

"I will. But honestly, I'm kind of hopeful that people will be glad to know about him as a man, not just as a victim this time."

"Like who?" Mika asked.

"Maybe descendants," I said. "I've been reading about Monticello and Highland, Montpelier, where the descendants of the people enslaved gather together to support one another and learn more about their shared history." I shrugged. "I may be aiming too high, but it sure would be nice to learn more about this man and be able to tell his family."

"Maybe Santi could do one of those forensic bone study things and find out what kind of work he did from the wear and tear. I hear some types of lab analysis can give us information on diet and water health." Mika's voice was getting higher and higher. She had a tendency to get very excited about the kind of police work she saw on TV. It was both hilarious and unrealistic.

"As valuable as this man was, I'm not sure the Octonia Sheriff's Department can drop that kind of cash to do a full forensic examination of his identity," I said.

She raised an eyebrow.

"But I'll ask, of course." I picked up my cup and stood. "I better get going, though. I promised to be home with dinner in a bit."

"Keep me posted?"

"Of course," I said as I waved and walked back onto Main Street. Our town was idyllic, at least on the surface, a quaint central street with shops and other businesses, hanging flower pots, and brick sidewalks. I loved living in Octonia.

But underneath all this prettiness was a hard history of pain for some of the area's poorest residents, including mountain folks who had been forced from their homes to make way for the Shenandoah National Park and, in fewer but still sizable numbers, enslaved people who had worked the small farms in the valleys around here. Farms like my own.

As I walked a couple of blocks to the old Victorian house that had been turned into the society's offices, I wondered about all the stories we were still too afraid to tell about where we lived. We had tales that were better kept private for good reasons, of course, but we also had collective stories of pain and oppression that could only be solved when out in the light of day. I had a feeling the story of this man was going to be one of them.

The offices of the historical society were comfortable and cool on this summer day, a condition that I knew they kept for the archival documents they housed but one I also appreciated since my short walk had made me sweat something horrible. I just stood in the cool air and let myself dry off a bit before going to find my friend.

As usual, she was up in the archival room at the long desk, an array of documents spread before her. "Paisley Sutton," she said as I walked in, "I was not expecting to see you today. What brings you in?"

"Mind if I sit down? It's hotter than blazes out there," I said.

"Of course, and please help yourself to a water if you need one." She gestured toward a small fridge.

"Thanks," I said and helped myself to one of the tiny bottles before I set it carefully away from the documents and sat down. "I have a new project, and I could use your help if you have time."

"For you, of course, I have time. How may I help?" She folded her hands on the table and turned her full attention to me. "I do hope you are not going to tell me this is about another murder."

I sighed. "I'm afraid I cannot offer such good news." I quickly got her up to speed on the location of the skeleton and what we knew of his identity, and then I said, "I think it's time I look into the history of my property."

"It does appear so," Xzanthia said. "What do you know?"

I shook my head. "Nothing, actually. I've done a lot of research on other people's places, including my neighbor's, but I've never even looked at the land records for my own."

"Well, we know they are the first place to start, so let's see what we can find on the county site, shall we?" She stood and walked over to a laptop at the edge of the room. Within moments, she had pulled up my GIS entry and begun to walk back through the land titles for the previous four decades.

She wrote a note with the last online title holder's name and said, "This is as far as the online documents can take us. Do you have time to go to the clerk's office?"

I glanced at my watch. "About forty-five minutes. Is that enough time?"

"With the two of us, I believe it will be," she said and closed the laptop. She then quickly turned off the lights, flipped the sign on the front door to closed, and locked up the building. "Lead the way," she said.

3

Most people only go to their local courthouse to pay fines or appear in court. I, however, had never been to a courthouse for either of those reasons. My trips were usually research-based, just like this one, and I loved being among the old documents.

Xzanthia took the slip of paper with the name we'd found from our online research and set it on the tall table in front of us. Then she pulled the appropriate index out and found the name. We were off.

Within a half an hour, we had traced my property back through two hundred years of ownership and come to the original builder, as best we could tell, Joel Mackey, who bought the five acres around my house for twenty-five dollars in 1847. The next title for the land in 1882 included mention of a house, so we made the leap that Mackey must have been the builder. And he was clearly the owner during the years that the man under my kitchen had been killed.

"Now you have a place to start researching," Xzanthia said as we packed up and headed out. "I'll pull the personal property tax records for you and see if Mackey is on there."

"Thanks," I said as we walked back up the street toward my car and the society. "Mind if I come in tomorrow to keep looking?"

"I'm counting on it. We have a murder to solve." Then, in the most informal and silly action I'd ever seen Xzanthia Nicholas undertake, she gave me a high five and headed off down the road. Clearly, she was as excited as I was.

WHEN I GOT HOME, all three boys were in the office putting in what was, apparently, the last of the baseboard. "Wow, it's beginning to look like a real office," I said.

"My desk is going to go right over here," Sawyer said.

"Oh, really? You have some important work to do?" I asked.

"I do." He was so serious, and it was so adorable.

"Well, then, you definitely need your own desk." I glanced over at Santi and then at my dad. "We'll get you one."

"Already under control," Dad said. "If you don't mind."

"Boppi has a desk for me, Mama," Sawyer said, putting a hand on my arm as if to comfort me. "So you don't have to worry about it."

I grinned. "Well, thank you, Sawyer. I appreciate having one less thing to worry about." I gave him a big hug. "Speaking of worrying, I'm a bit worried that Beauregard might eat all our Chinese food if we don't get inside to eat what I brought home."

Sawyer raced toward the door and then stopped short. "Did you get me egg rolls?"

I snapped my fingers. "Shoot, I only got enough egg rolls for Santi and me."

"Oh, Mom," my son said with a wave of his hand. "You're so silly." Then he headed toward the house without looking back.

"I'll be on my way then, Silly Mom," Dad said as he gave me a quick hug. "But I'll be back in the morning to finish the trim and see if we can't get these walls mudded."

"Thanks, Dad. You don't mind?" I knew the answer, but I also knew that one of the greatest slights I could give to my dad was presuming help without asking. Only arrogant, "big-headed" people did that.

"Of course not. Eight in the morning work?"

"Sure thing, Mr. Sutton," Santi said and walked my dad to his truck.

When Santi returned, I said, "You guys okay to handle things tomorrow? I was hoping to get a little further in my research."

"Absolutely," he said. "Not really enough room for three of us to move in there anyway." That wasn't exactly true, but I appreciated the kind lie. "Find anything today?"

Just then, Sawyer charged into the kitchen, making monster truck sounds all the way before coming to a stop with a screech of his "tires" in front of us. "Washed my hands. See?"

I did see. I saw dirt on the back of his hands and the wet stain on his shirt, but I mostly saw his effort. "Nice, buddy. Thanks for doing that. Ready for your egg roll?"

"Yum," he said and licked his lips with enthusiasm. "Did you get cashew chicken?"

"You know it," I said as I fixed his plate with an egg roll, a fair helping of cashew chicken, and a couple of pieces of broccoli from Santi's beef and broccoli. Whether or not he'd eat the broccoli was a toss-up, but I felt obligated to at least put something green on his plate.

As we all sat down, Santi and I exchanged a look that made it clear neither of us was going to talk about the skeleton with Sawyer. He'd eventually find out—our community was small, after all—but until we knew more and could answer some of the many questions he would have, we both knew it better not to say anything.

Instead, we talked about Sawyer's newfound love of the nail gun. Apparently, Dad had let him use it, under careful supervision, Santi assured me, and Sawyer now wanted one of his own. "Maybe Santa will bring me one?"

I knew better than to let this idea grow, but this was a delicate subject—Santa Claus—so I said, "You know, Santa prefers to give toys. Maybe you could think of a toy you want more?"

That did the trick because Sawyer immediately said, "The Jurassic Park Jeep that I can ride." From there, he told us all about the tricks he would do in the yard, everything from wheelies to headstands, and by the time he was done, I wanted to get him the Jeep and a full array of body armor to protect himself.

"Seriously, Saw," Santi said, "You should be a stuntman."

"What's a stuntman?" Sawyer asked as he carried his cleared plate to the counter without me asking.

"Well, a stuntman takes the place of an actor and does all the dangerous stuff like big jumps or car crashes," Santi said. "Want to watch some stuntmen on TV?"

"Stuntwomen, too?" I said.

"What about non-binary stuntpeople?" Sawyer asked.

"Those too," I said with a smile. It was a blockbuster night. Sawyer had eaten, cleaned his place, and naturally asked about gender diversity. I decided I would revel in my superb parenting for a moment with a can of hard cider while the boys watched stunt videos on YouTube.

I cracked open my cider and my laptop at the same time and sat down at the table. I wasn't surprised at all to see a message from Xzanthia in my inbox. The subject line was "PPT Files." I opened it and saw right away that she had found a record for Joel Mackey and that, in 1867, he had three Black men working for him—Isaiah LeVarge, Luke Johnson, and Thames Mathis. There wasn't much hope I'd find Luke Johnson, as his name was just too common. But Isaiah LeVarge and Thames Mathis had names that were unique enough to warrant a search on the genealogy sites. If we found out our victim was one of these men, it would prove he wouldn't have died enslaved, but since formerly enslaved people often continued to work for their previous owners even after the Emancipation Proclamation, it was possible he had been enslaved by Mackey at some point.

I couldn't resist the temptation to dive into research immediately, and the minute I put in Isaiah LeVarge, I got a hit in another user's family tree. They traced their family line back to him, seven generations from the youngest person in the tree, a woman whose name I couldn't see because she was still alive. Still, I could drop a note to the tree's creator and see if they responded.

My message was short. "I have information about the property where Isaiah LeVarge worked in 1867. I'd be happy to share if you're interested." Hopefully, I'd hear back.

Unfortunately, Thames Mathis's search wasn't so easy. His name didn't show up under that spelling on any records, so I figured one of two things had happened. Either his name had been misspelled on the personal property tax records, or he had changed his name in some way, maybe just the spelling or maybe the whole thing. Either way, he was going to be harder to find.

I decided to table that research until the morning and turned my attention to tidying the kitchen. I was just finishing up when my phone rang. It was Claire. "Hi," I said, trying to sound cheery and not nervous, even though a call from my only employee after six p.m. made me quite nervous.

"Hi, Pais," she said with what sounded like excitement. "I just wanted to update you on what Horatio Denver bought today, and he also has a question he wanted me to ask you."

"Oh yes, please," I said, sitting back down at the table. "Do tell."

"Well, he bought all the stained glass. Said it was too beautiful not to scoop it up, and he paid almost full price for the whole lot." She was obviously quite pleased with this bit of news.

"Wow," I said. "That's amazing." Amazing enough to almost guarantee that Sawyer would get that Jeep from Santa, in fact.

"Yep, but that's not all. He wants the two oak mantels, and if you don't mind him taking off one wall and reselling you the unused logs, he wants the cabin at the front of the lot. He said he wanted to use it as the kitchen on his client's new house." Her voice was breathy, and no wonder. That was almost twenty thousand dollars of merchandise in one sale.

"Holy cow," I said in my own whispery voice. "Wow." I was at a loss for words. That was my single biggest sale ever.

"Well, there's more," she said. "He was looking for an old chicken coop, not to buy but to model after, and I know yours is probably original to your house. I told him I'd ask you if it was okay for him to come out and see it."

"Oh, sure," I said. "When does he want to come?"

"Tomorrow, if possible," she said. "Apparently, his client is quite eager to get everything moving."

"Fair enough, and I'd be eager to take advantage of that enthusiasm if I was Denver, too. I'll be out in the morning, but if you want to tell him he can stop by after one, I'll be sure to be here."

"Great," Claire said, and we ended our conversation.

I walked into the living room and motioned for Santi to join me in the kitchen. I'd learned that talking money in front of Sawyer was not wise because he thought ten dollars and ten million dollars were roughly two dollars apart.

As quickly as I could, I told Santi what Claire had just said, and he gave me a hard hug. "I know that's a weight off your mind."

It was. I had taken a loan from Mika's Uncle Saul to get our office up and running, and while I'd been making regular payments and the loan had no interest, I was eager to be free of that debt, and today's sale would make that possible. "I'm so excited, and this means we can hire a band for the wedding."

We'd talked about that possibility, but the cost was prohibitive. Now we could have folks dancing.

"We could," Santi said, "and we will if you really want to, but I don't know that our folks are really dancing folks, and they'd probably be just as happy with some recorded music coming through a speaker."

I leaned against his chest and thought for a minute. "You're right. Let's figure out what to do with the money this weekend. Right now, I just want to enjoy this feeling."

As if on cue, my son said, "Mama, come see this."

I walked into the living room just in time to see what looked like a 1988 Crown Victoria jump approximately 856 other cars in a mud pit. "Whoa," I said.

"That's what I'm going to do," Saw said as he rubbed one eye with his still chubby fist.

"Oh yeah. I thought you were going to do research," I said as I sat next to him on the floor and pulled him into my lap.

"I can do both, Mama," he said as he nestled into me. "You always say I can do whatever I put my mind to."

"You're right, Saw. You absolutely can."

THE FOLLOWING MORNING, with Saw safely at school and Santi assuring me that he wouldn't let my dad work too hard in the incessant heat, I headed over to meet Xzanthia and show her what I'd found.

Of course, as usual, she was already one step ahead of me and had done some of the primary source research to locate Thames Mathis. She had found a man named Thomas Mathis in the census records from 1870, but before she moved forward with the assumption that this was the same man from the property tax records, she wanted me to look.

I scanned the census record, looking at both the information about Mathis and his family and the data about his neighbors. I was absolutely sure that Xzanthia had done the same thing, and when I saw the name Mackey two listings up from the Mathis listing, I was sure we had the right guy.

"You saw they were neighbors of the Mackeys?" I asked with a smile.

"I did," Xzanthia said. "So we agree that this is our man?"

"I believe so," I said and held up my hand to see if I could get another of my friend's spontaneous high-fives. When she smiled and turned away, I had my answer. "Now, do we think his name was actually Thames or Thomas?"

"I had the same question," she said, "and I think it's Thames."

I was strangely excited by that fact, maybe because I was just a fan of people with odd names like my own. And like Xzanthia's, for that matter. "What makes you think so?"

She pulled the laptop over to the table and opened her online collection of records. "So here's a marriage record for a man named Thames Mayes. He looks to be about the right age, and he's Black."

I scanned the document and made a few notes about his father's name and his wife's name, Bertha Bennett. "Got it," I said.

She opened another doc. "And this is a birth certificate for his son, Thames Mathes, spelled with an *e*, from two years later."

I made more notes as Xzanthia continued through three more documents that seemed to confirm that the man who worked for Mackey in 1867 was named Thames Mathis or Mathes.

"I could have kept going," she said, "and I will later. But I didn't want us to get distracted from our real purpose here."

I nodded firmly. "Right. We are trying to identify the man

who was buried under my kitchen." I was glad that Xzanthia had stopped because I knew all too well how deep I could get into one line of research only to be on a total tangent from what I had originally been seeking. "So, we know that the man who was buried under my building was about thirty-five years old." Alex had texted that fact over to Santi just this morning.

"Right, so I don't think it was Thames," Xzanthia said. "He was only twenty-four when he got married in 1868."

"Yeah, so it's possible it could be him, but only if Alex missed the mark."

"Have you ever known Alex to be off by that much on anything?" She raised an eyebrow.

"No. No, I have not. But we also can't rule him out entirely. We know that slavery was hard on a person's body, so it's possible the man we found was actually younger than his bones implied." It wasn't a fact I liked to ponder—that the experience of enslavement might have aged a person by a full decade—but I knew it was highly possible.

"Fair enough," Xzanthia said. "But I do think we have another good option." She clicked open another document, a birth certificate for a woman named Ivy LeVarge.

"Oh my. Is that Isaiah LeVarge's daughter?" I asked as I scribbled down names and dates.

"Indeed. And she was born in 1876." She closed that document and opened a page of notes. "I can't find a marriage certificate for LeVarge and Miriam, his wife, which means they may not have been legally married according to the Commonwealth."

I sighed. "Okay, so what makes you think Isaiah might be the right person?"

Xzanthia's face broke into a wide grin. "This." She clicked over to a newspaper article from the local paper, and on the screen was a photo of a tall, thin Black man with a white mustache and white hair. The caption said, "Isaiah LeVarge wins county fair pumpkin contest." And sure enough, right there next to him was a hip-high pumpkin.

"Holy cow," I said and leaned in to look at the date. "1926." I frowned. "But that can't be him. The man buried at my house was dead by"—I did the math quickly in my head—"1890 at the latest."

The smile on Xzanthia's face grew wider. "That's because this man is *our* Isaiah's son."

"Oh, he's a junior?" I asked.

"Or maybe a third or four or fifth. Could be that name was passed down for generations." She tapped a few keys, and a family tree popped up. "And here, there's an Isaiah LeVarge who died in 2003."

I looked at the name of the tree's owner. "I wrote that person last night." Quick as a flash, I had my phone out and my email open. Sure enough, there was a response from the owner. I clicked over to the genealogy app on my phone and read the message.

"I am Isaiah LeVarge, the eighth, and I'd love to hear what you've found," his note said and included an email address. I read the message aloud to Xzanthia.

"Oh, my gracious."

"If nothing else, Paisley, I think we've found some living descendants with ties to your property," she said. "But I think it's quite possible that the man found at your house was Isaiah LeVarge."

I couldn't disagree with her, but I was a bit stymied on how to prove that. "I agree, and yet, it could have been Thames Mathis, too. Or even Luke Johnson."

"And it could have been another man altogether." Xzanthia put her hand over mine. "We need to take our wins here, Paisley. We may not be able to positively identify the man buried at your place, but we can make his death serve a purpose and give some families back their histories." She squeezed my fingers.

I took a deep breath and said, "You're right. I'll reach out to this living descendant, and if it's all right with you, I'll invite him to meet me here." I sighed. "We're almost done with my office, and I'd hate to have him come and see where his ancestor's resting place was when it was under construction."

"Plus, maybe we could get a small memorial to all three of these men to put outside your office?" She looked at me with hope.

"Oh, I love that idea. Let me put Mika on that. I think she knows some engravers, and we'll make a plaque big enough to add names later if we need to do so." I reached over and hugged my friend. "Thanks for your help."

"Of course. I'll keep digging and let you know what else I find." She waved to me as I walked out of the archive room and back to the street.

A quick glance at my watch told me I had just enough time to stop in and see Mika before I picked up subs for Santi and Dad. Fortunately, Mika was more than happy to coordinate getting the brass plate manufactured, and I texted her the names we needed on it for now. Then I dashed into the corner gas station, got three of the best sub sandwiches in the world, and headed home to write Isaiah LeVarge VIII.

4

While I was away, Dad and Santi had mudded all the walls and proceeded to cut a hole in the newly finished back wall to put in a surprise for me—the French doors I had dreamed of having.

"What?" I shouted as I walked in to tell them lunch was here. "That looks amazing." And it did, but I was a little overwhelmed by both the gesture and the expense. Santi and I had agreed that the doors just weren't in our budget for the time being. I shot him a concerned look.

He came over, hugged me tight, and whispered, "It's your dad and Lucille's wedding gift to you, but he doesn't want you to know that." He stepped back. "They look great, don't they?"

I swallowed back my tears and nodded. "They really do. I love that you found ones without any mullions. I love the open view to the back field." They were exactly what I had dreamed, a view and also a way to let natural light into the room. "Thank you both so much." I gave Santi another hug, and then I nearly squeezed the breath out of my dad as my silent thanks to him and Lucille. "Now, who wants IGA subs?" Oddly enough, our tiny grocery store made the best sandwiches.

"You don't have to ask me twice," Dad said with a bit more rasp in his voice than usual. As he turned away, I saw him wipe a tear from his eye, but I knew better than to make any mention of it. He was a tender man, but he didn't like for anyone to recognize that.

JUST AS WE were finishing lunch, a dually pickup pulled into my driveway, and I remembered that Claire had said Horatio Denver was coming by. I washed my hands and quickly gathered our trash before heading out to meet him.

"Hi, Horatio," I said as I put out my hand to shake his. "I hear you want to build a replica chicken coop." I pointed toward the back of the house as we walked that way.

"I do. I could just construct something, but I want it to feel old." He smiled at me. "And as you know, if you want something to feel old, it needs to be old, or at least be like old."

"I do know," I said. "Well, this is my beauty. Take pictures, measurements, whatever you need. We'll just be over here"—I pointed to the office twenty-five feet away—"finishing up our project."

"Perfect. Thanks, Ms. Sutton," Horatio said as he took his phone out of his pocket and began circling the building.

I stepped back inside the office and marveled at the doors once again as Dad and Santi put the final trim around the frame.

"Any new updates on our friend from below the floor?" Santi asked. "Sorry, was that insensitive?" he asked with a wince. "I just don't know what to call him. Skeleton seems too awful, and victim defines him by what someone else did.

"You can call him Isaiah because I think that might have been his name," I said with a look from Santi to Dad.

Dad whistled. "You identified him?"

"I don't know for sure that this person was Isaiah LeVarge,

but Isaiah fits the right age and time frame. I'm going to write to his eight-times great-grandson today and invite him to look at what Xzanthia and I have found."

A scuff at the door alerted me that someone was behind me. I turned to see Horatio in the doorway, his mouth slightly open. "Did you say Isaiah LeVarge?" His ears turned a little pink. "Sorry for eavesdropping. Isaiah's my partner."

My chest got tighter. "Oh, really. Wow. Well, I was just going to email him." I wasn't sure how much Horatio had heard or how much he should hear. The fact we may very well have found the skeleton of his partner's ancestor under the building we were standing in felt like too much to casually share at the moment.

"Forgive me for asking," Santi said as he walked up and shook Horatio's hand. "When you say partner, do you mean—"

Horatio interrupted him, "I should clarify. He's my business partner, but we are also married." He held up his left hand and showed his wedding ring. "So partner in both senses." He smiled.

I liked this man, and not just because he had given me the single best sales day in my company's history. He seemed genuine and kind and had a great sense of historic preservation, which always gave someone bonus points in my book. "Is Isaiah around today, by chance?"

Horatio turned his chin up a bit and looked at me more closely. "He's on a project just over in Barboursville. I can call him and ask him to join us if you'd like."

"Really? That would be great." I spoke before I looked at Santi, but when I did, he was nodding.

"Yeah, we have some news for him, and it would be good if you could stay. He might want your support," Santi said.

Horatio took out his phone. "I'll call him right now, but I have to admit that the way you're talking is making me a bit apprehensive."

"Sorry," I said. "It's just that we should tell Isaiah what we need to share first. It's about his family." I didn't feel like I could say more, but maybe that would alleviate Horatio's fear a little.

Horatio nodded and then stepped outside to make his call. A moment later, he came back in and said, "Isaiah is on his way."

My heart started to pound. I had imagined I'd talk to the descendant of the man buried underneath my new office via email and then in the calm space of the historical society. The fact that he was coming here, to my home and the potential site of the murder and the burial site of his ancestor, made me quite nervous.

I looked over at Horatio, who was staring out across the fields below, and reminded myself that this guy was quite lovely, and chances were that his husband would be too. Plus, the two men who loved me most in the world were here to support me. I could do this.

Still, I wanted Xzanthia to be involved in this conversation if she could be, so I gave her a quick call, told her what had happened, and asked if she could join us.

"I'll be there in twenty minutes," she said and hung up. I was glad she'd been to my house before since she hadn't waited to get an address or directions.

A few minutes later, I heard tires on the driveway and walked around the front of the house with Horatio to meet Isaiah. He was a tall, dark-skinned man with a goatee and small gold hoops in his ears. He was a bit dusty, probably from a work site, but he wore khaki Carhartts and a polo shirt, the uniform of the preservation community as I thought of it—dressed up enough to be professional but also practical for climbing into attics and under porches.

Horatio and Isaiah hugged briefly, and then I stepped forward. "I'm Paisley Sutton. We corresponded, I think, online."

A sudden flash of fear coursed through my limbs when I realized I might have been talking to someone else.

"We did," Isaiah said. "I'm glad to meet you." He looked from me to Horatio. "But I am very curious about why you called me out here. Do you mind explaining?"

I nodded. "Of course. Let's go back this way." I told them a little bit of the history I knew so far about the house as we walked past the creamery and toward my office. "This building was the summer kitchen. It's very likely that an enslaved woman cooked here, maybe even lived in this building."

I paused and let the men take in that bit of information. Talking about the history of slavery was sensitive, and although I'd done it a lot over the past few years, I was still aware that people had strong reactions to both the places and the stories that dealt with that part of our shared history.

"We're now converting it into my home office while trying to preserve the integrity and history of the building." I led the way inside while Santi and Dad stood by the French doors at the back. "We're leaving the ceiling as-is because I want the marks from the smoke and soot to remain, and we've kept as much of the original floor as we could."

The two men looked over the space and then rested their gaze on the floor. This was the moment.

"When we were repairing the floor two days ago, we found a skeleton under the building." I hadn't meant to be quite that direct, but there it was.

"A skeleton?" Horatio said. "Whose skeleton?" His face drained of color even as he asked his question, and he looked over at his husband.

"We are not absolutely positive," I said, "and probably never can be." I looked at Isaiah. "But we think it might be your eight-times great-grandfather, Isaiah LeVarge."

A muscle flicked in Isaiah's jaw, and I saw his chest swell as he took a large breath. "Okay," he said slowly. "Can you walk me through how you think that's possible?"

"Absolutely," I said. "Xzanthia Nicholas from the historical society is on her way over, and we can show you everything. Would you like to see where we discovered his remains?"

Isaiah nodded slowly, and Santi stepped forward and gently lifted the trap door he had put in when we laid the floor. We felt it had been a way we could honor that this space had been someone's grave since moving the building wasn't an option, given that such a move would probably destroy this building and the stories it could tell.

Isaiah stepped forward and knelt down by the hole. Beneath, I could just see the edges of the white lilies we had laid there for Isaiah. I couldn't put a tombstone up for him, but I could remember him with flowers.

Horatio came forward and put his hand on his husband's shoulder, even as Isaiah reached down and tucked the tips of his fingers into the earth. He stayed that way for a long while, and Santi, Dad, and I stepped out to give the men some space.

I heard Xzanthia arrive and walked around to meet her at the front. I told her that Isaiah was at the burial site and asked if she'd like to go back. When she nodded, I led the way, and she stood just outside the door with her head bowed while we waited.

The two men came out a few minutes later, and I waited for them to speak first. "Thank you for remembering him," Horatio said. "Would it be possible for us to bring something small to place on that site?"

Isaiah looked at me expectantly.

"Of course," I said. "Absolutely, and I'll give you a key to the office when it's done so that you can come and pay your respects anytime."

"Thank you," Isaiah said. "Where is his body?" he asked very quietly.

Santi said, "It's at the coroner's office, and once the full autopsy has been completed, we can release the body to you for burial."

Isaiah nodded and looked at Horatio, who dipped his chin just once. "Would it be possible, Paisley, for us to reinter him here?" Isaiah said. "Not under the building, obviously, but in a proper grave."

A few years ago, I would have had to consider that request carefully, mostly because of concerns about legality and such, but given that my father had decided he wanted to be buried on his own land and had done the investigation to be sure that was possible, I now knew that in Virginia, with certain considerations, people could still be buried legally on private property.

"Of course," I said and turned to face the back of my two acres. "What if we created a small memorial space and gravesite by that tree there? He'll be on the land he knew but also in private enough space that you and your family can come to visit anytime without needing to interact with my son or us."

Isaiah looked toward the large oak at the back corner of my land. "That is perfect," he said. "And you're right by the train, which my grandfather and father love. I expect they'll find that fitting."

I smiled. "Excellent. Just let us know when you're ready for the interment, and we'll have the equipment and necessaries for the burial." I knew Saul would be happy to come out and dig the grave. "Would you like to have a ceremony?" I asked. "No pressure to decide now. But if you do, you are most welcome."

"Thank you," Isaiah said as he looked back into the office. "If it's okay with you, I'd like to learn more about what you've found and how you identified my grandfather."

"Of course," I said. "This is Xzanthia Nicholas, the director of the Octonia County Historical Society. She and I can walk you through what we found."

Horatio, Isaiah, Xzanthia, and I headed toward the house
while Dad and Santi headed out for a walk. I was so glad they
intuited that continuing to work on the office wasn't a respectful
idea at the moment.

Inside, I poured us all glasses of sweet tea, and we sat
around my kitchen table with Isaiah beside Xzanthia. She set
up her laptop and opened the genealogy site before beginning
to explain the path we'd taken to find out who had worked on
this property and who might have been buried under the
kitchen out back.

When she was done, Horatio said, "So it's not certain that
the man was Isaiah, *my* Isaiah's grandfather."

"Not completely certain, no," Xzanthia said. "But when
you've done this work as long as I have, you learn two things—
leave room to change your understanding but take what understanding you have as truth when it's the best you've got."

That was my way of thinking about research, too. Some
historians wanted to pin down every fact and solidify every
detail with some sort of paper trail. But when it came to the
lives and stories of enslaved people, that just wasn't possible—
at least, not in most cases. The fact that we could suppose
Isaiah LeVarge worked here for the Mackeys and then surmise
he was the right age to be the man buried beneath the kitchen
was a great deal more than most people knew about any
enslaved person. It wasn't enough. We would never be able to
find enough information or recover enough stories honoring
the humanity that these people were denied for so long. But
both Xzanthia and I believed that honoring what we could was
more important than certainty.

Isaiah nodded. "Even if he's not my relative, he deserves a
proper burial. No matter what, we'll take care of that." He
glanced over at Horatio, who nodded. "How can we help figure
out what happened to him?"

I sighed. "I so appreciate you asking," I said. "The sheriff,

Santi, my fiancé"—I pointed back toward the kitchen—"has made it clear that he wants to find out what happened to Isaiah and solve the murder, but of course, the means he has to do so are limited, given how long ago the murder took place."

Isaiah put up a hand. "You keep saying murder?"

"I do because I cannot think of another possible reason that a person would be buried underneath a building, particularly a kitchen." I hoped that everyone at the table could infer what I meant by that and we could avoid a conversation about the process of decomposition. "Plus, we did recover a knife, and the coroner saw evidence of a stabbing on the skeleton."

"Whoa,' Horatio said. "He was stabbed to death?"

I took a deep breath and nodded. "It appears that way. I don't know the particulars from the autopsy, but the coroner will include those in her final report."

"And you said you found a knife?" Isaiah asked. "What kind of knife?"

"It looked like a boning knife, maybe, one of those thin ones that people use to gut fish." I winced at my description, but it was accurate. "Santi can probably tell you more."

The men nodded. "So what else can we do?"

"Well," Xzanthia replied, "do you have any family records, or is there someone in your family who specializes in keeping the family's history?" She looked at Isaiah expectantly.

"Actually, yes. My cousin Mary, Mary Jackson. I'm sure she could help."

I grinned widely and smacked my hand on the table. "Mary is your cousin? I swear that woman is kin to everyone in Octonia."

"You know her?" Isaiah said.

"Know her? She's one of my best friends. We did the work on her church together. Do you go there?"

"Nope, my daddy's family goes over at St. John. But what a small world." Isaiah's face had relaxed a bit, and he was smiling.

"Well, let's get together with Mary and see what we can figure out."

"Great. Want to gather here tomorrow afternoon?" I asked. Sawyer was going to his dad's right after school, which meant we could talk into the evening if necessary.

"That sounds great. We'll bring drinks," Horatio offered.

"Thanks. And I'll ask my stepmom to make some snacks for us," I said and then paused. "Do you feel comfortable having her and my dad—you met him out back—Santi and our friend Mika here as well? They've done a lot of this kind of research before and know a lot of people from Octonia. They might be able to help us piece things together."

Isaiah smiled. "The more, the merrier." He held my gaze for a minute. "Just so you know, Paisley, I'm proud of all my ancestors, and while the fact that some of them were slaves is painful, it's not a pain I want to avoid. This is our history"—he gestured around the table—"and I want people to know it."

I reached over and squeezed his arm. "You are in charge here," I said. "Whatever you are comfortable with, we will do, and if there's ever anything you'd prefer not to be shared or such, please let me know."

"Actually, you write a newsletter, don't you?" Horatio asked me as he slipped his arm around Isaiah's shoulder. "Babe, what do you think about Paisley writing up what we find tomorrow and seeing if other people can provide more information?"

Isaiah nodded. "I love that idea. If you wouldn't mind, Paisley."

"I wouldn't mind at all. In fact, I'm honored you asked. I'll start putting the story together today and finish it for Sunday's newsletter." I glanced over at Xzanthia. "Do you want a version for the historical society bulletin?"

"If that's okay with you." She looked over at Isaiah.

"Definitely. The more people who know, the more we can find out." He actually seemed a little excited now as he stood up. "I have to get back to the job site, but I'll see you all tomorrow. See you at home." He kissed the top of Horatio's head and headed out the door.

After Isaiah left, I looked at Horatio. "You okay?" I asked.

He shook his head. "I'm not really sure, but if he's okay, then I'll get there, too. Look, I didn't want to say this in front of him, not because it's a secret but because he's kind of embarrassed by his interest in family history, but he has been looking for a long time to find information about his direct line."

I tilted my head. "I thought Mary was the family historian?"

"She is, but Isaiah is, too. They work together a lot, and they've found a ton of information but mostly about uncles and aunts, not his direct ancestors. So this is a big deal." Horatio ran a hand over his hair. "I'd really like to make tomorrow special, so if you let me, I'll have dinner brought in for everyone, along with drinks. And I'd like to bring supplies we might need. What would you recommend?"

I stared at him for a minute. I'd been hosting impromptu research parties for a couple of years now, and we usually sat around with laptops and glasses of wine to sip when we weren't scarfing down frozen pizza. This was a change.

Horatio looked so excited and expectant, and I didn't want to disappoint him. "Actually, a large whiteboard would be really good . . . and markers for it. Maybe you could bring your laptops if you have them?"

"Definitely. What else?" He looked at me like I'd just asked him to bring a few spare paper clips when he wanted to supply a rocket ship.

I closed my eyes for a minute to imagine what I wanted the time tomorrow to feel like, and I went with whatever images came to mind. "Colored Post-it Notes in lots of sizes, some yellow legal pads, smooth-writing pens—"

He interrupted me. "What brand?"

"Uniball Vision Elite," I said without hesitation.

"Great," he said as I heard his pen scratching on paper. "Now what else?"

"Maybe a couple of gift subscriptions to the genealogy site so that everyone can get on and work at the same time?" I opened my eyes and looked at him nervously. I hoped I hadn't gone too far.

"Perfect," he said as he finished his notes. "Consider it done. If it's all right, I'll come around noon to help get everything set up. Do you have tables and chairs?"

I glanced down at the table in front of us. "Besides these, no."

"All right, I'll bring folding ones. Maybe we can set up workstations in the living room?"

I smiled. "Excellent. Thank you," I said.

"Honestly, it's the least I can do. Isaiah has been looking for so long." He stood up, and when I followed suit, he said, "Do you mind if I give you a hug?"

I put out my hands. "Bring it in," I said and immediately blushed because I realized I had settled fully into middle age with that expression.

The huge man squeezed me tightly and then walked toward the door. "Oh, and by the way, the chicken coop is perfect. I've got everything I need to replicate it, and I'll send your finder's fee over to Claire later today." He stepped out the door and headed toward his truck before I could even speak.

"A finder's fee?" I finally said to Beauregard, who was staring up at me with an expression as baffled as my own. "For the building that holds my chickens?"

I looked at Beau again, but he was already bored by this conversation and had moved over to take up the prime yowling position by his food bowl.

The good mood of the day was catching, so I opened a can of tuna for him. We were sharing the wealth today, that was for sure.

5

I loved my son with a fierceness I could not have even imagined before he was born, but on the weekends, when he went to his father's, I experienced a kind of lightness that I just couldn't have when he was nearby. For one, I could sit down in the evenings for more than five minutes at a time, and the burden of keeping at least half of myself ready for him lifted. I was always a little sad, too, but I'd learned just to let the sadness go through me and use the time when he was away for the things I needed and wanted to do without the presence of a small human.

Genealogical and historical research was definitely something better done without the "assistance" of a small child, as was anything involving fragile objects. Hence, I was at my shop Friday morning to help load Horatio's items, including the eight stained glass windows he'd purchased.

Saul and his crew were experts at loading things, and I knew they would be especially careful with the glass. But it didn't feel right for me not to be onsite today. After all, this was my biggest single sale ever, and given what Horatio was contributing to our work today and my new tie to his husband's family, I just wanted to be there.

When I arrived at eight, the crew had already loaded up everything but the windows because they had begun work at six thirty to avoid the heat of the day. One of the guys was now using the small crane to lift the first window over the truck. The pieces had to stay upright in order for them not to break. Laying them down would shift the weight and separate the lead, and then all the windows would have to be repaired.

So Saul's crew had created an upright rack like the ones on glass trucks to carry the windows. The uprights of the rack were made from two-by-fours attached to a heavy wooden base that was, in turn, bolted to the truck bed. Once each window was loaded, they would carefully use ratchet straps to secure the wooden frames around the windows to the rack and then drive slowly to Horatio's job site in Crozet to unload.

"Looking okay, boss?" Saul said as the second window flew slowly through the air toward the truck.

I nodded. "Your team is doing great, but this is nerve-racking."

Saul laughed. "Don't worry, Pais. We'll get everything there intact." He slung an arm over my shoulders. "Your dad told me at breakfast about what was happening this afternoon. Mind if I come over? Not sure what I can do, but this seems important, and I'd like to be a part of it."

"Of course, Uncle Saul. And also, if you won't mind, we're going to reinter the remains at my house. Could you or one of your guys bring over an excavator and dig the grave when the time comes?"

"You don't even have to ask, Pais. Just let me know when and where, and we'll be there." He squeezed me. "All right, I'm going to ride along on the trip and be sure the unloading is smooth. What time this afternoon?"

"Anytime after one is great. We'll have food and drinks, and

Horatio is supplying everything else we need, too." I still couldn't believe how generous he'd been. This morning, two new laptops arrived at my house by courier. "Gifts for the team," the note had said. "See you later," I said to Saul as I walked back toward my shop.

Claire was inside, this time hanging brightly colored ribbons from a wrought-iron weather vane and turning it into a beautiful piece of art. "Man, I want you to go back to school next semester, but I'm very glad to have you around. You do good work, woman."

She beamed at me. "Thanks. I saw something like this on Pinterest and wanted to give it a go. This weather vane is so pretty by itself"—she tapped a finger on the galloping horse's head—"but it kind of disappears against the wall. Thought this might draw some attention to it."

"Definitely," I said. "That is one of the downsides of the salvaged wood. It isn't as bright as a white wall would be. That looks amazing." I had no doubt someone would buy that this weekend when they came in, and they'd probably want to use it as wall art now.

"Everything loaded up for Horatio?" she asked as she stepped off the ladder.

"Almost, and Saul is going along to supervise the unloading." I sighed. "That makes me feel a bit better. We're responsible for the items until they touch the ground at the site, and I really, *really* don't want to break up anything that Horatio is planning to use."

"I hear you there," she said. "Did he tell you about his plan for the windows?"

I shook my head. "I'd love to hear, though."

She took out a sheet of paper and sketched what looked like a window wall in a timber-framed house, a vision I knew well from my own dream-house plans. Then, she sketched some smaller panels and colored them in with red and blue pens and yellow highlighter. "See, most of the wall will be transparent, but then he's interspersing these windows for texture."

"How big is this wall?" I said as I glanced back toward the truck where the massive stained glass pieces were being tied into place.

She shook her head. "He didn't give me exact dimensions, but apparently, it's enormous. He said the house was going to double as a wedding venue, so I guess this might be the ballroom or something?"

I looked down at her picture again. "I'm going to need to see this in person when it's done," I said. "Maybe he'll give us a tour."

"Ooh, that sounds great." She turned and tapped a few keys on the register. "He also sent a check for a thousand dollars, and it's labeled chicken coop. Did he buy yours?"

"A thousand dollars! What? No, he just took pictures and measurements. Gracious." I couldn't believe this man. "That's very generous."

She smiled. "I get the feeling he likes being generous, and from what I can see on their website, business is good for them. They're remodeling houses for some of the celebrities around here." She opened a screen on the tablet beside her and pulled up an image of a massive farmhouse that a local author was renovating. "This one is 8,500 square feet plus a massive horse barn."

I studied the picture and let go of a little of the guilt I was holding about how much Horatio had paid me. The guilt wasn't reasonable anyway—I hadn't overcharged him in any sense—but the fact that he had very high-end clients confirmed that he was quite aware of what my pieces were worth and could afford them. I suddenly felt kind of giddy. My business was growing.

"You need anything for the rest of the day?" I asked my fully capable staff member out of habit.

"I've got it. Need me to focus on anything in particular?" Claire asked.

I was hit with a spark of inspiration. "Actually, yes. Could you take a couple thousand and find items related to the experience of slavery? Nothing gruesome or related to the torture and imprisonment of people, of course, but maybe some hand tools or plows from that era?"

"I can definitely look and see what folks might have. Are you looking to resell those?"

I shook my head. "Nope. I want to make a little museum on the working history of enslaved people here in the back room." I pointed to a space that used to be a parlor of sorts but was now only used for storage. "Something to remember their contributions to our local architectural history."

Claire smiled. "I like that idea. I'll see what I can find. Want me to compile some possibilities for you?"

"Yes, but also, grab what things are appropriate and available now if you can be fairly sure they're tied to the labor of enslaved folks," I said. My giddiness was spurring new ideas, and I wanted to go with them ASAP.

"I'm on it. I'll let you know what I find." She smiled, turned back to her iPad, and began searching immediately. I might have to give her a raise.

"Thanks," I said and jogged out to my car.

I drove to the historical society to pick up a couple of boxes from Xzanthia so that I could get them sorted and ready before people arrived that afternoon. When I walked in, I stopped short. Someone was shouting in the archive room, and they were not using polite words at all.

Without hesitation, I took out my phone and texted Savannah, "Need you at the historical society now." Then I ran up the steps only to find a tiny White woman with her chin almost in Xzanthia's chest and a finger waggling at her face.

"Stop spreading lies about my family. We are good people.

Always have been. We treated those folks fair and good. But all you—"

I interrupted her as the n-word flew out of her mouth. "Ma'am, you need to step back and watch your language," I said as I walked over and stood shoulder to shoulder with Xzanthia. "You okay?" I said to my friend without looking away from the hateful woman.

"Is she okay?" the tiny woman with a head of curly black hair said before Xzanthia could speak. "What about me? That post"—she turned back to Xzanthia—"implies that my family was mean to their slaves. We were no such things. We were good slave owners."

I turned my eyes toward Xzanthia, and I could see she was composed but barely. Her jaw was tight, and the look in her eyes was something I had not seen before—real fear. "Miss, I don't know who you are or what you are talking about, but you need to speak to the director with respect, first of all. Second, there were no such things as good slave owners. There were only people who were crueler than others to their slaves. That's a fact and one we won't discuss further here." My voice was steady, but I was full of rage.

The woman widened her stance and turned to me. "Look, I don't know what you think you know, but my family has been in this county for—"

I didn't let her finish. "My name is Paisley Sutton, and my family has also been here for several generations. You don't get to pull that card with me. More importantly, you don't get to pull it with Ms. Nicholas here. She knows more about the history of this county than the two of us will ever know." I took a deep breath and heard the door to the house open at the same time. "Now, if you would like to discuss something about the historical society with Ms. Nicholas in a calm and respectful manner, I'm sure she will be willing to assist you by sharing her extensive knowledge, but if you insist on assaulting this woman and using hate speech against her, I'm sure Deputy Watson here will be happy to escort you out." I looked over the woman's head at Savannah, who stood in the doorway, both hands on her hips.

"That's right, Ms. Mackey. As I explained this morning when you came to the station, Ms. Nicholas and the historical society have not broken any laws. You, however," she said as she walked toward the three of us, her hand still resting on her gun, "are dangerously close to being arrested for harassment." She stopped in front of the woman and waited.

I don't think Ms. Mackey knew what to do with two strong Black women and a strong White woman standing up to her bullying because she sputtered a bit and then looked down at the floor. "We aren't bad people," she finally said more calmly.

Xzanthia extended a hand toward the table behind Ms. Mackey. "If you'll sit down and speak to me calmly, I'm sure we can discuss this situation."

Ms. Mackey looked at her and then dropped into the closest chair, which happened to be the one at the end of the table. I sat down next to her while Savannah stayed standing near the door. Xzanthia then made her way the few steps to the other end of the table and took a seat, meeting Mackey's power position with her own. Gracious, I loved that woman.

"Now, please bear with me, Ms. Mackey, as I catch Ms. Sutton up on what has transpired. I believe you are familiar, Deputy Watson?"

Savannah nodded, and then Xzanthia turned to me. "Paisley, I posted on our social media accounts this morning and told people a bit about Isaiah LeVarge and our suspicions that he had been enslaved here in Octonia by the Mackey family."

"See what I mean?" Ms. Mackey said, her voice louder again.

Savannah stepped closer to the table, and Mackey sat back

against her chair. This time, though, she didn't lower her eyes. She wasn't backing down from this.

I took out my phone and pulled up the historical society's Facebook page to read the post. It was, almost verbatim, what Xzanthia had just said. "So, Ms. Mackey, you are a descendant of the Mackeys who owned my farm." This wasn't about me, but I thought maybe I could divert a bit of her ire my way.

"You own my grandparents' old place?" she asked, her eyes wide.

"If you mean the place they owned back in the 1850s, then yes," I said. "If you ever want to visit, I'd be happy to show you around."

She looked at me, and her mouth opened and closed a few times. "Well, thank you." She looked at me another minute and then turned to Xzanthia. "Now, see, that's a reasonable way to speak to someone. You could take a note or two."

Xzanthia simply folded her hands in front of her and kept her mouth shut.

I, however, was out of patience with this woman. "I do not know what you think Ms. Nicholas has done to you, but you are in no position to lecture her on manners, not after the names I heard you calling her." I leaned over and got my face very close to hers. "I am happy to talk with you about your family history, and knowing my friend here, even though you have been ultra-hateful to her, I bet she will too. But neither of us will do any such thing if you keep giving us this nonsense about how you and your family have been wronged. Are we clear?"

Ms. Mackey stared at me for a long minute, her eyes bulging, and then she said, "All right. Can I ask a question?" Her tone was still haughty, but at least she wasn't shouting.

"Sure," I said as I sat back. "What would you like to know?"

"How did you know my family owned slaves?" At least she didn't deny the facts.

I looked over at Xzanthia and said, "Would you like to answer that, or would you prefer I did?"

"I'll be happy to answer your question, Ms. Mackey," she said as she stood up, picked up her laptop, and came to sit across the table from me on the other side of Ms. Mackey. She tapped a few keys and then spun her keyboard to face the head of the table. Then, methodically and clearly, she showed Ms. Mackey the title records for the property that she had photographed at the clerk's office. Then she pulled up the personal property tax records that we had used to identify Isaiah LeVarge and the two other men. Finally, she opened the 1860 Slave Schedule from the US Census and showed Joel Mackey as owning four slaves.

I hadn't seen that last document yet, but the numbers reflected what I had surmised. Joel Mackey had owned a small number of enslaved people, probably the three men from the tax records and likely one of their wives.

"So, while we cannot one hundred percent prove your grandfather enslaved LeVarge, Johnson, and Mathis, we do know that he did indeed own four slaves and perhaps more," Xzanthia concluded.

"This is private information, not something people should be able to look up," Mackey said softly.

"It's all public record, Ms. Mackey. Available about any White person living at that time," I said.

"Right, but Black people owned slaves, too," she spat with a tone that made it sound like she thought she had us there.

"They did," I said, "because it was sometimes a way to acquire wealth. But often, formerly enslaved people or free people of color bought their own relatives to keep them from being sold or sent out of state." We could have given her a lot more information about slave codes that required people to leave the state after they were freed and such, but mostly, I just wanted her to be aware that we had heard all the legends and lies created to dismiss the horrors of slavery. We weren't going to be sidetracked by misinformation.

"Ms. Mackey, what does your family know about that history?" Xzanthia asked after a moment of letting the information I shared sink in. "It seems you know your family enslaved people. Is that common knowledge among your family?"

Mackey looked at Xzanthia and then turned her gaze to me and said, "Joel Mackey was a good man. He taught his slaves to read and write, and he gave them jobs after they were freed by the War of Northern Aggression."

I had to fight very hard not to roll my eyes at the tried-and-true Confederate sympathizer term for the US Civil War. But I fought down my urge to correct her narrative in favor of getting information that might prove useful to Isaiah and his family.

"I see," I said with a glance over to Xzanthia, who gave me an encouraging nod. "Do you have any records about him? Maybe he kept a journal or something?"

"Oh, we have lots of papers, and yes, I think it would be a very good idea for you to get both sides of the story here. I'd be happy to let *you*"—she looked pointedly at me—"borrow them if you promised to care for them."

Well, here was a gift I hadn't expected to receive today. And I knew the cliché about the horse and the mouth. "I will take very good care of them. Any chance I could come with you now to get them?"

Ms. Mackey frowned a bit.

"I'm just really eager to get as much information about your family as I can, especially since they owned my house." I was treading a fine line here. I didn't want to lie, and I certainly didn't want to encourage this woman's racism or deluded historical beliefs, but her family papers could very well be rich with information about the people they enslaved.

"All right then. You can follow me to the farmhouse. They're all in a sealed tote. Old papers have to be kept at a constant temperature and away from moisture, you know?"

She was heading toward the door past Savannah, so I shot my two friends a wide-eyed look. Xzanthia smiled, and Savannah stifled a laugh behind a cough. "Of course, Ms. Mackey. Of course, they do," I said before I mouthed, "Pray for me" to my friends.

THE RIDE to Mackey's farm was short. She lived on one of the roads that turned off Main Street toward the mountains. It was a lovely farmhouse set on a small rise with a gorgeous view of the mountains. But like many farmhouses around here, it had seen better days. The paint was faded and peeling, and the corner of the porch was held up by an old fence post.

Clearly, this family didn't have the financial means to take care of what was obviously a beloved home place. "My great-grandmother's peonies," Ms. Mackey said as she pointed to bushes that flanked either side of the concrete steps up to the porch. "They have the prettiest pink blossoms in May."

"I bet they do," I said. Peonies were one of those old-time flowers that everyone had at their old homes around here, but they had also become really trendy for city people. A friend of mine cut her stems, put them in her farmstand each May, and charged five dollars a blossom. She saved all that money and bought her kids' Christmas presents with it, saying she had her granny to thank for all the toys lying around her living room.

The inside of the house was like a time capsule. The wallpaper, though faded and peeling in the corners, was the shade of blue that well-appointed historic houses were always trying to reacquaint. And the woodwork was gorgeous and obviously handcrafted. Even the art seemed to be old, primitive-style portraits of people I assumed were part of the Mackey family. "Wow, the history in here is amazing."

Ms. Mackey's face lit up. "I've tried my best to keep things up," she said, "but it's just me—never had any children—and my brothers don't really want anything to do with the old place. I keep hoping one of my nieces or nephews will take an interest before it's my time."

For the first time since meeting this woman, I felt a pang of sympathy for her. She really did care about her family's story, and she must have felt very alone in preserving it. I could see how the combination of loneliness and racism had led to her reaction to Xzanthia's post.

"I hope they will," I said. "It really is a beautiful home."

"Thank you, dear," Ms. Mackey said. "The records are here in the library." She led me through a doorway on the right into a red-enwrapped room with floor-to-ceiling bookshelves. It was something out of a book lover's dream.

"Wow," I said as I turned in a circle. "What a library," I said. "Are the books original?"

"Most of them," she said with a twinkle in her eye. "I do my best to preserve them well, but it's hard in an old house. I've actually thought of selling some of the collection just so it's preserved."

I wondered if the proceeds from that sale might help her do some of the repairs around her house. "I have an acquaintance who owns a rare bookshop down in Charlottesville. He appraises individual books and collections like yours. Would you like me to put the two of you in touch?"

Ms. Mackey put a hand to her heart. "You'd do that?"

"Of course," I said. "I'll give him a call this weekend and share your number with him if that's okay."

"Please," she said and wrote her phone number on a piece of light blue notepaper on the top of a small desk by the window. "I'm available almost any time for him to come out."

I folded the paper and slipped it into my pocket. "I'll let him know."

She smiled and then turned to a clean blue tote beside the desk. "Here are the family records we have." She bent down and slid the tote out. "If you'll carry this one, I'll pull out the other three."

"Other three? You have four totes full of family papers?" This was a treasure trove indeed.

"I do, and I've organized them by year, just like they do in formal archives." As I picked up the first tote, she tugged another two out from behind the long curtains. "If you don't mind carrying them out, I'm not as strong as I used to be."

"Of course," I said. I was sort of shocked by how this woman's demeanor had changed since this afternoon. I wasn't naïve enough to miss that she related much better to White people, but I also wondered if she might feel a bit more heard than she had this morning. It was amazing how simple attentiveness could soften a person.

6

When we got all the totes loaded into my Subaru, I thanked Ms. Mackey, told her I'd get everything back to her ASAP, and headed out. As soon as I was out of her driveway, I called Mary to see how prep was going on her end.

We'd talked the night before, and she was very excited about getting together with everyone, even if the news of her ancestor's body had been a bit of a shock. Now, though, she was in full research mode. I could hear it in her voice as soon as she answered. "Pais, so I've got all my binders as well as links for all my family trees. Plus, my cousin is bringing over the box of papers she's been wanting me to go through so we can put that in the mix for today." She was talking so fast that she was out of breath.

"That all sounds great, but I have one question. Have you eaten yet today?"

The silence on the other end of the line was long. Finally, though, Mary said, "No, I haven't. I need to do that." She let out a long whoosh of breath. "I'll do that. You know how I get."

"I do know, and that's why I asked. Take a break. Grab some

food. Maybe walk around your yard for a few minutes?" I smiled at the phone. "You do realize we can keep going tomorrow if we need to, right? It doesn't all have to be done today."

"Right. Right. It doesn't have to be done today." I could hear her breathing deeply. "That helps. Thanks, Pais. All right, I'm going to take that walk. See you at two."

She hung up, and I smiled. Not many people in the world got as excited about history and genealogy as I did, so I was glad to have met Mary. And I was lucky to have family and friends who were super supportive of what I did. That was a rare gift, for sure.

When I got home around eleven thirty, Santi and Dad had just finished sanding the office. Both of them looked like they'd been dipped in powdered sugar, so I sent Dad home to clean up and recommended Santi do the same. Then I pulled out my stash of paper plates and plastic utensils, gave the kitchen a wipe down, and made sure the furniture was at least relatively free of Beauregard's hair.

When I sat down next to my fluffy guy on the couch, I decided I should probably prep him for what was coming. I had no idea if he understood any human words beyond *hungry* and *treat*, but if he did, he deserved to know his house was about to be full.

"Beauregard, we're about to have friends over to do some research. That means there will be lots of paper and lots of food. You know the rules—no shredding, no peeing, and no begging. Got it?"

He stared at me sleepily.

"Now, would you like to stay here, or would you like me to put you upstairs on the bed?"

He set his head back down on his paws and closed his eyes. Clearly, I had my answer.

Given that Beau was not going to be moving from his spot

on the corner of the couch, I was glad that Horatio was bringing folding chairs because we would need them. I just hoped no one was allergic to cats.

I was fretting in the middle of the living room when Santi came down from getting dressed. "You okay?" he said as he came over and hugged me. "You're just staring at the couch."

With effort, I pushed a smile onto my face. "I am, but I just hit the stage of 'nothing left to do to prepare,' and I'm stuck."

"Well, here's an idea. Why don't you go sit on the porch, and I'll bring you a cup of tea to sip until Horatio arrives?" he said and walked me to the front door.

I took a deep breath as I sank into the rocker. Just in the last year, I'd realized I had some real anxiety and perfectionism issues, especially when it came to having people in my home. I'd begun to work through a lot of my conditioning around my expectations of myself. But today, a lot of that mess was coming up again.

As I rocked on the porch, I realized it was because I felt like a lot was at stake. We wanted to find out, definitively if possible, if the man whose skeleton we'd found was indeed Isaiah LeVarge. Then I wanted to figure out what happened to him. But I was also invested in my friends, new and old, and finding what they needed. As Santi handed me my cup of Earl Grey, I realized that some of my anxiety was coming from that very question—what did Isaiah and Mary want to find through this research? I decided that would be my first question for everyone when they arrived.

Santi and I sat quietly on the porch for a few minutes, watching the finches dance around in the field below. Then a car pulled in, and we both stood, nodded to one another, and went around the house to meet Horatio.

And he had come fully loaded. Today, his truck was packed with tables and chairs, and in the front seat, I saw a couple of cases of beer and several bottles of wine. But it was the catering van that pulled up behind him that really caught my attention. He had hired The Pie Guy, my favorite food truck in the area, to cater, and I was thrilled. I couldn't wait to eat one of their mushroom pies, but I was ready to sample everything. These hand-sized pies were the best things in the world, and they were at my house.

When The Pie Guy himself stepped out of the truck, I almost squealed. I'd met him at a couple of events, but here he was in my driveway. I wondered briefly if this was how those teenage girls had felt when they saw the Beatles perform. Luckily, I managed to contain myself, shook the man's hand, and then began to help carry things in.

Within a few minutes, my kitchen smelled divine, and my house was staged and ready for an afternoon of work and conversation. The Pie Guy—who I was sure had an actual name, but I was too nervous to ask about it—headed out after setting us up, and I was sad to see him go.

But once I bit into one of his sausage rolls, I kind of forgot about the man himself and just savored the food.

Apparently, I looked like I was enjoying myself because when I came out of my butter-inspired stupor, Santi and Horatio were staring at me and smiling. "That good, huh?" Santi said.

"Oh yeah. That good," I replied with a smile. "All right, what else do we need to do?" I put down the rest of my roll reluctantly.

"You're the boss," Horatio said, "but maybe we could get the materials set up in the workspace."

"If by *workspace* you mean my living room, then yes." We had already put up the tables and chairs, so Santi started to set up the free-standing whiteboard that Horatio had brought. It was the size of the ones you would find in classrooms and was perfect.

Horatio and I began setting out legal pads and pens, and

then I got the guys to help me bring in Ms. Mackey's totes. "I think we need to have workstations for each set of papers," I said. "I don't want to get any of them mixed up."

"That's a good plan," Horatio agreed. "Let's put all of Ms. Mackey's stuff here at this table, and then we can use this one for Isaiah's stuff. Sound okay?"

I nodded. "Mary's bringing papers, too, so maybe she and Isaiah can share the table since their records will probably intersect."

Santi moved two chairs behind each table. "It might be wise for you to think about having assignments ready for folks, Pais. They're going to look to you for guidance, and we all know how it feels volunteering to help and not having a clear task to do."

"Sure." I picked up one of the markers from the tray at the bottom of the whiteboard and wrote three columns: LaVerge/Jackson, Mackey, and Online. Then I quickly wrote names below each heading. Mary and Isaiah would obviously work on their family papers, and I thought maybe Saul could help them. Then I assigned Xzanthia and myself to the Mackey files, with Dad helping us. That left Lucille, Horatio, and Mika to online tasks, which I thought was great. They could be the go-betweens for the groups and look up specific questions while also making notes about things on the whiteboard. "Does that look okay?" I asked the two men.

"Looks great," Santi said, "except I don't have a job."

I blushed and laughed. "Oh, yes, you do. You're our police expert. I'm hoping you'll see what you can put together about the murder itself. You know, do your thing."

"Alrighty then, and with that in mind, I have some, well, I won't say *good* news, but you'll see what I mean." He reached into his satchel, sitting on a stool by the kitchen counter, and took out his laptop. "I got the autopsy report this morning, so maybe Alex was able to figure out a bit more to guide us."

"Well, yeah, that is goodish news." I stared at his laptop. "Have you read it yet?"

"I haven't," Santi said. "I wanted to wait until Isaiah and Mary were here so that I could tell them first."

"That's very considerate," Horatio said.

Santi nodded and set his laptop on the trunk by the window, claiming his seat. Horatio did the same by setting his own computer on the end of the sofa next to Beau. The cat was, surprisingly, pleased by the presence of a new human and lifted his head and began purring when Horatio scratched his chin. I chose to take that as an auspicious sign for the success of our day.

The three of us took pies and drinks and headed to the front porch to wait for everyone else to arrive. The heat was pretty intense today, but the humidity was relatively low as we sat and rocked, an act of grace for which I gave audible thanks. All that moisture in the air made Virginia's summers so brutal.

"Not to pry," I said after a few minutes of comfortable silence, "but is Isaiah doing okay? That was a big surprise yesterday."

Horatio looked out over the field and said, "It's kind of you to ask. Yes, I think so. We talked last night, and he had a lot of feelings that he needed to move through, but he's mostly just really eager to find out more."

"I hope we can find out more today," I said, my anxiety kicking up just a bit because there were no guarantees in this kind of research.

"Me, too," Horatio agreed, "but I also think there's a lot to be said for a group of people who care enough to really explore this with us. Thanks for that."

I took a long slow breath and let my thoughts gather. "For a long time, I think we've sort of decided that doing things on our own was the best way, that asking for help or doing things together was weaker, less efficient or something. But we are always stronger together. The work is always better, and it's always more fun, too."

"I miss church potlucks," Santi said. A person who had not grown up in a southern church might not have understood the way that idea connected, but both Horatio and I "hm-hmmed" our agreement. Potlucks were quintessentially communal both in the giving and the receiving. And they were beautiful for that. Well, for that and the macaroni and cheese.

My thoughts drifted to the spread of food in the kitchen, and I was just about to head in and get some of that amazing macaroni and cheese I'd seen, but a car came down the driveway.

"That's Isaiah," Horatio said and headed off to greet him.

Soon enough, more cars pulled in, and when Lucille and Dad arrived, I ran out to help carry in the four plates of goodies Lucille had made. She had recently developed a gluten intolerance, so two of the plates were gluten-free goodies—brownies and lemon bars—that I knew from experience were just as good as the chocolate chip cookies and magic cookie bars she'd made. Nothing was bad, of course. Not at all.

By the time everyone got inside, the house was bustling with activity, and I saw Santi go over and push down the thermostat on the AC a few degrees. I gave him a hearty two-thumbs-up for good thinking because it would get very warm in here soon if we didn't compensate.

No one hesitated to scoop up the scrumptious food Horatio had provided, and a few people grabbed beers or glasses of wine to go with it. I knew the alcohol would flow a bit more freely as soon as the day got a bit further along, but I was glad to feel comfortable getting my own glass of white wine, too. It was going to be a long day in a lot of ways, and I enjoyed the way alcohol soothed my nerves a bit.

Once we all got seated, our drinks carefully tucked on coasters far away from our papers—something Xzanthia monitored well—and our hands clean of any buttery residue, the room got very quiet, and everyone turned to look at me. Santi had been right. I was in charge.

"Thank you all for coming," I said as I pushed myself to stand again. "As you can see from the whiteboard, I've taken the liberty of assigning us each a focus. We have a lot of documents to peruse, so I thought it best we divide up the work."

I explained the roles of each group but also stressed that we should be communicating regularly about what we find. "This is a big puzzle with a lot of pieces, and if we don't talk to one another as we go, we won't solve it. So if you find something you think is relevant to the Mackeys, Isaiah and Mary's family, or anything that seems to speak of murder around our time period, please share."

"Paisley," Mika said, "could you post some dates for us? Give us some parameters."

"Oh, that's a good idea," I replied and jotted up 1847 for the date Joel Mackey bought his farm. Then I speculated 1850-60 for the building of the house. From there, I put up all the dates we knew about Isaiah LeVarge and the other men who were working for Mackey in 1867. It was a sparse time line, but it was a time line. As the backbone of our research, it was helpful.

"Anything else you need that would be helpful?" I asked.

No one said a thing, so we all dug in. As I sat down, I heard Mika say she'd dig into the newspaper records, and Horatio said he'd work with Isaiah's family tree on the genealogy chart. True to form, Lucille volunteered as a gopher and assistant anywhere she was needed.

Santi took his laptop over to where Mary and Isaiah were sitting and faced it toward them. As they silently read, I saw tears spring to Isaiah's eyes. I couldn't even imagine what it must have felt like to read about your ancestor and his murder. I breathed a quick prayer of comfort for him.

But then I saw Xzanthia had already pulled out a tote, removed a folder, and stuck a bright pink Post-it on the folder behind it to mark her space. I needed to get rolling too. Four totes full of paper was a lot of reading.

It took a while for anyone to come up from their research to share anything, but it was Xzanthia who found our first good bit of information. "So, according to these notes in Joel Mackey's ledger, he bought supplies for his house in early 1850, and the purchases stopped by the end of that year. So we can surmise safely that the house was finished in 1850."

Lucille stood and modified the building date entry on the whiteboard. "Any other dates we need to add so far?" she asked.

"Birthdate for Isaiah LeVarge the third is 1852, according to his death certificate," Mary said.

"Isaiah the third. So are we thinking that's the man in the newspaper photo?" I asked.

Mary nodded. "That's what the dates imply, yes."

"All right, now we're cooking with gas," Saul said with a smile.

"We are," Xzanthia agreed. "Now we can tentatively put the date of birth for Isaiah the second—the man who was murdered—as 1830."

Lucille wrote the date up and then asked, "Why can we surmise that?"

"Because in genealogy work, we often assume that the age a person has their first child is around twenty. Of course, he could have been younger or older, but that gives us a range to pinpoint his birthday," Xzanthia replied.

"Got it." Lucille made a list that began with Isaiah number one and continued through Isaiah number seven. Then she wrote in their birthdates, including the birthday of the man in the room with us—1979.

Saul studied the board for a minute and then said, "There's a pretty big gap between Isaiah three and four. I know a man can have a child much later in life, but his wife would have to be younger, wouldn't she?"

Mary slapped her hand on the table. "Uncle Saul, I think you've found the next question we need to answer. Let's go."

Saul grinned and tucked my rocking chair up to their table. They were on their way again.

THE ENTIRE AFTERNOON and evening went that way—a discovery, a conversation, a new avenue of inquiry. We were a focused group, even as the alcohol started being consumed more quickly, and at eight p.m., everybody was tired but eager to continue, myself included.

However, the law of diminishing returns is a real thing, and fatigue exacerbates it, so we called it a night shortly after nine with a plan to regroup here at nine a.m. with coffee and bagels provided by Horatio again. When his husband said, "And donuts," a small cheer went up from the crowd. We were grateful for bagels, but we were giddy for donuts.

After the last car pulled down the driveway, Santi and I collapsed onto the couch with Beauregard, who had not moved except for the brief moments when he had convinced Mika to feed him—because he was absolutely famished, of course.

Santi had been very quiet all afternoon as he huddled over his laptop and tapped into his phone, and I was quite eager to hear what had kept him so focused. He'd only had one beer, and while my fiancé wasn't a big drinker, he usually had two on a night like tonight. Either he was so focused he forgot to drink, or he chose not to drink more because he wanted to stay focused.

"So, do you think it would be okay if you shared the autopsy with me?" I asked, fully aware that he had both professional and personal protocols in mind here. He might toe the line when it came to police procedure, but he would never break a person's confidence unless absolutely necessary. Telling his fiancée what the findings were was not absolutely necessary.

"Sure. Mary asked if I would, but she didn't want to talk about it today with everyone. She and Isaiah wanted to sit with the findings a bit before we introduced them to the group. I assured them that was fine because, first of all, I didn't think the group would have much to contribute to the murder investigation as of yet and because their feelings mattered most, of course."

I kissed his cheek. "You're such a compassionate guy," I said. "Now give me the laptop." I playfully tugged it out of his hands.

"Yes, ma'am," he said as he let it slide over onto my lap and then stood. "Chamomile?"

"Oh, that would be lovely, with lots of honey, please."

"Deal, but when you're done reading that, we are going to watch something mindless, and you are going to sew, okay?" He winked as he went into the kitchen.

I didn't mind that requirement at all. I was making good and steady progress on my new project, an image of single flowers in blue glass jars. It was fairly simple as projects went, and I hoped to have it done and ready to hang before the wedding. Of course, that timeline had been in place before we found a body under my office, but I was still hopeful.

When I opened Santi's laptop, the autopsy report was open on the screen, and I quickly scanned it. I didn't understand a lot of the medical terms, but I could see that the man had been stabbed two or maybe three times with a thin-bladed knife. I wasn't surprised by that information, given what we already knew.

But the next few paragraphs did give me pause. They

described severe osteoarthritis in his knees and hips and a substantial amount in his shoulders and elbows as well. The phrase "consistent with repetitive tasks of manual labor" drew my attention, as did, "This individual had injuries and degeneration to his bones consistent with someone who had worked with heavy objects for many decades, perhaps a mason."

I set the laptop on the bookshelf beside me and stared straight ahead at the purple light outside the window. "He was a mason?" I said when Santiago sat down.

"Looks that way. That's what Mary and Isaiah wanted time to look into. Apparently, they have a long line of masons in their family, so they wanted to see if they had any records that backed that up," Santi said as he handed me my tea.

"And did they find anything?" I was getting really excited again.

"We are done talking about work, right? Tomorrow will be here soon enough. I need to know if Romeo gets his act together." He turned on the TV and navigated to our third episode of *Bachelor In Paradise*. The show was terrible in all the best ways, and I was surprised by how playfully invested Santi had gotten. By the time we went to bed two episodes later, Romeo had been eliminated, and we were quite pleased about that decision.

7

When the alarm went off the following morning, I was bleary-eyed and groggy and was hit with the very rare temptation to snooze, but even as I hit the button and settled back into my pillow, my brain fired the synapses to say, "Research Day," and I was awake and in my favorite yoga pants and T-shirt before my alarm went off again. Research days were my favorite days.

I quickly checked in with our new part-time clerks for the shop to be sure they were all set for the day. Randy was going to be going to the City Market with our booth, and he assured me he was already there and finishing the display. Claire sent me a voice text to say she was on her way in now and would have the store open by ten. I let a little of my tension for the day ebb away. My business was still going, even when I wasn't there. That was a new feeling.

Around eight thirty, my phone went off, and Mika surprised me by saying she was on her way. "Mrs. Stephenson is covering the store again, so I'll be there in five. I brought you a latte."

"Bless you," I said. I was very grateful for the coffee Horatio was drinking, but this day required at least one shot of espresso.

My best friend knew me very well, and she had asked them to double-pump the vanilla. It was a perfect jolt of sugar, cream, and caffeine.

Shortly after Mika arrived, Horatio and Isaiah pulled up with a dozen bagels and two dozen donuts. Clearly, Isaiah had talked some sense into his husband. They also brought boxes of locally brewed coffee from the Orange Coffee Roasters, and when I saw them pull oat milk creamer out of a grocery bag, I almost hugged them.

As people arrived, they got their breakfast and chatted a bit, but everyone seemed pretty eager to get back to work, so we all settled into our spots in the living room, Beauregard included again.

We'd been working a few minutes when Mary asked for everyone's attention. "We have some good information that we want to share about Isaiah the second," she said with a glance toward Isaiah, who took over.

"First, we are almost one hundred percent positive that the man under the office was my great-grandfather, my namesake." He went to the whiteboard and flipped it over. "We know the birth dates for my father and grandfather, and we're pretty sure we've found birth and death dates for my great-grandfather as well." He wrote those years up on the boards.

"Now," he continued, "we first need to realize that we have a missing generation here." He pointed to the space between 1852 and 1909, the time they speculated his great-grandfather had been born. "From census records, we know that a man named Isaiah LaFarge was born in 1882." He looked around the room as only a man comfortable with public speaking can do and said, "so obviously, that's my third great-grandfather, Isaiah LeVarge. Thank goodness for standardized spelling, right?"

Everyone chuckled.

He went on. "So, it looks like there are eight in total with this name." He tapped the board with his blue marker. "That's the first thing." He pointed to Mary, who joined him at the board.

"Have you guys practiced?" Lucille asked.

Mary and Isaiah exchanged a look and then laughed. "Nope. Must be genetic," Isaiah said as he sat down.

"Now, according to the autopsy of Isaiah the second— maybe to help keep everyone straight, we'll just call him Kitchen Isaiah since he's the man who was buried back there." She gestured toward the back of the house. "That Isaiah's body was severely arthritic, and the coroner speculated that he did manual labor all his life. That fact alone isn't surprising for a man born into slavery and then living in its aftermath. But the coroner also suggested that his joints indicated that he might have been a stone mason." She paused for effect.

Everyone stared at her before looking at Isaiah, who nodded in support. "That's right, y'all," he said with a smile.

"Here's where it starts to get really personal," Mary said before clearing her throat and continuing. "My granddaddy was a stone mason, and Isaiah's granddaddy was a stone mason. Their daddy, Isaiah, was also a stone mason, and while we don't know about the grandfathers before them, we imagine they passed down the trade."

Tears welled in my eyes. "So, what you're saying is that you've traced your family line back eight generations, and most if not all the men were stone masons. Am I getting that right?"

Mary met my eyes, and I saw her tears. "That's right."

The whole room was silent for a few minutes until Xzanthia spoke. "Well, that makes what I have to share almost anticlimactic, but I found records in Joel Mackey's journal that he was a stone mason."

"Whoa," Dad said. "Did Kitchen Isaiah learn from him?"

Xzanthia shook her head. "Nope. Looks like he was trained at a plantation." She took a deep breath. "Before he got his own land, Mackey was an overseer at a place down in Fluvanna

County, a big place called Bremo, if you know it. There, a stone mason named Peyton Skipwith taught Isaiah the trade."

A sort of awed whisper passed through the room.

"Peyton has a building named after him at UVA, and he was also one of the masons who helped build the rotunda there. So your ancestors learned masonry through the lineage of another enslaved mason," Xzanthia said with a little rasp in her throat.

By this time, I was crying, as was Mika, and even Saul looked a little choked up. This kind of information just wasn't available to many descendants of enslaved people. And to have that many generations back with a trade that was passed down was super rare. Usually, this amount of detail about a family was only discovered if the ancestors had been enslaved on a famous plantation, like the presidential homes of Madison and Jefferson. I had never heard of anyone having this kind of history for a family on a small farm like the Mackeys.

"But the best thing I've found," Xzanthia said after a quiet moment, "is that I have positive proof that Joel Mackey enslaved your ancestor, Kitchen Isaiah, for a full fifteen years. In fact, I think it's safe to assume that Isaiah probably laid the foundation for the house we sit in right now." She took photocopies of a document and passed them around the room. "Here, Joel Mackey talks about hiring Isaiah out for mason's work. It looks like he and Mackey worked side by side on a lot of projects around Octonia."

Each of us stared at the paper in front of us, a page from a ledger showing wages brought in from both Joel and Isaiah in 1855 for masonry work at the "old church."

"Do we know where the old church is?" Mika asked with excitement.

"Not yet," Xzanthia said with a smile.

I looked over at Santi as he stood up and began clapping. "That is so impressive. You've just identified a body, friends.

Good police work," he said, "but more importantly, you've given that man a name and a story. That's amazing."

Mary grinned. "It is amazing, and I can't believe we know so much about it." She took a deep breath. "We don't know why he was killed, though. I'd like to know that."

"I would, too," Santi agreed. "So let's keep looking." He glanced over at Xzanthia. "I take it you haven't gone through all the Mackey papers yet."

"Not even close," she said. "We've maybe covered one box between the two of us."

"Well, let's all switch to working on that," Isaiah said. "Does that work?"

I smiled. "Of course, just know that the wrath of Ms. Mackey will come down on us if we damage any of her family papers," I said with a smile, even though I was only half joking. I didn't think the woman would be thrilled to learn that Black people had been looking through her family's history, but I also didn't intend to tell her.

"Why don't you, Dad, and Mary take this box?" I said as I pulled one of the totes out from beside me and carried it over to their table. "Mika, Lucille, and Horatio, you want the other one?"

When they nodded, I grabbed the other box and handed it over. Soon enough, we were all elbow-deep in Mackey family papers. My box hadn't yielded much so far. I had picked the second tote in the chronology, so most of my records were from the 1870s onward. I didn't expect we'd find much after the years Xzanthia's box covered—1800 or so to 1869—but you never knew. I'd seen historical reminiscences that named enslaved people and talked about where they lived that had been written well into the 1930s.

Even as we worked, I was struck yet again by the painful irony of the fact that to research enslaved people, you had to delve deeply into the history of the people who had held them as property. Because the White male owners were the people who had both wealth and social status, not to mention legal standing in society, they had the most historical records. And, of course, we know history is almost always told from the victor's side, those with the most power. So to even begin to recover the truth of the experience of enslaved people, historians had to go deep into the stories of the people who enslaved them, and I hated it.

But life was full of things I hated that yielded good things, like summer giving way to fall and my child's temper tantrums leading to snuggles, so I buried myself in this awful work, too. About an hour later into our day, Horatio said, "I think this might be relevant." He went to the whiteboard and wrote, "Octonia Man Says Father Was Murdered."

"What? Is that a newspaper article?" Mary asked.

"Yep," Horatio said and began to read. "At church on Sunday morning, fourteen-year-old Isaiah LeVarge III told the congregation that his father, Isaiah LeVarge II, had been murdered the previous Friday night." Horatio continued to read the article, and apparently, the teenager had asked for the congregation's help in identifying the two men who had killed his father. The boy said both men were White and had stabbed his father three times in the chest with a boning knife.

Horatio stopped reading. "That's the whole article. It was clipped and in a folder with some letters from Joel Mackey's grandson, Jefferson. But I read all the letters, and nothing at all mentions the murder or anything about the LeVarges at all."

"What date is on that article, Horatio?" Xzanthia asked.

"October 7, 1878," he said. "Which means Isaiah was probably killed on the fifth, right?"

"Seems right to me," I said as I stared at him for a moment and then looked over at Isaiah. "You haven't heard anything about that at all?"

Both of them shook their heads. "Not a word," Mary said,

"and I've interviewed all the elders. No one mentions one of our ancestors being stabbed to death."

"Maybe they didn't know?" Horatio said.

"Or maybe there's a reason they kept it a secret," Isaiah commented with a long glance at Mary. "I'm thinking maybe we need to take a trip to see Auntie Bess, don't you think?"

"Seems so," Mary said. "Coming to church tomorrow? Maybe we can convince her to go eat?"

"I like how you think," Isaiah said before he turned back to the rest of us. "That's pretty specific, huh? The knife, the three stabs, the two men."

"And it lines up with the coroner's account," Santi said. "But what doesn't make sense is that if this young man saw his father get stabbed, why was his body not buried formally? Wouldn't he have gone to his dad, even if he'd waited until the attackers left, to see if he was okay?"

"With all due respect," Isaiah said, "I know you're a Brown man, but right now, you're thinking like a sheriff. Do you think a Black boy during that time would have run outside after he saw his father killed, even if he thought the attackers were gone? I doubt it. And maybe the men took his dad's body and put it under the office. Maybe no one could find it."

Santi nodded. "You're right. I hear you. But, and forgive the gruesomeness of this fact, the body would have started to smell, so wouldn't that have led them to look for it?"

Xzanthia shook her head. "Not necessarily. It might have been dangerous to do so. After all, depending on who the men were, it might have been risky even to recover the body." She shuddered. "It's horrible to think about, but survival was paramount then. That's how we made it out of slavery. We survived."

My throat was tight, but I didn't want to cry. No one needed to deal with my White woman's tears as they talked about the things their ancestors had needed to do to stay alive. I swallowed hard and nodded. "So then it might be really useful to figure out where the old church was, see its history?"

Mary nodded. "I was just thinking that. I haven't seen any mention of a congregation by that name in our church records, so I don't think we came out of there." Mary was her church's historian, so she would know.

"Let's list the other Black churches then," Horatio suggested as he stood up and went to the whiteboard to write down the names as people shouted them out. By the time our list was as complete as we could make it, we had ten churches, not including Bethel, the one that Mary and Isaiah attended.

"You can cross off Evergreen, too. That's my home church, and as you can imagine, I know our history pretty well. No mention of the "old church" there either," Xzanthia said.

"So that leaves nine," I said, more processing to myself than really sharing with anyone else. "I can call all the church secretaries," I said as I recalled the advice Xzanthia had given me previously about who really knew what was going on at local churches.

"Paisley, just say the word if this doesn't suit, but we could invite folks here for a genealogy day, maybe next Saturday?" Mary suggested.

I glanced at Santi, who was already nodding. "That's a great idea," he said. "Give us a chance to talk with everyone at once." He looked over at me. "That's okay with you, right?"

"Of course," I said, and it really was all right, although it made me very nervous. "The only problem I see is that my house is so small, and I only have one bathroom." We were already testing the capacity of that one small room with this many people here today.

"Oh, we can handle that," Horatio said. "I'll rent a tent and have some porta potties brought in."

I stared at him for a minute and then nodded. "Okay. And

maybe we could invite a couple of food trucks out so people can get lunch?" Now I was starting to dream big.

"That's a great idea," Mika chimed in. "Maybe the historical society would like to set up a table to answer questions and get members?" She looked over at Xzanthia, who was nodding.

Lucille spoke quietly and said, "This may be too much, but I've heard of other organizations doing photography days where they bring in pictures to have them digitized, and then the pictures are put online so people can identify the individuals."

"I love that idea," Isaiah said. "We have a couple of high-quality scanners we can bring out, with a generator for electricity," he said with a smile at me, "and I can mock up a quick website."

The ideas were coming quickly now, and I could barely keep up. Apparently, though, we were also going to hold the interment ceremony for Isaiah II that day, as well. Saul said he and his crew would prepare the site this week and serve in whatever way the family wished for the service.

"Let's make it open to everyone," I said as the plan was settled. "But let's only formally invite folks through the Black churches, okay? We all know what can happen at this kind of event if it doesn't have the right focus, and I just can't handle the Confederate flags on my property."

Santi came over and put an arm around me. "I think that's a good idea, and I'll make sure we're all on duty that day just in case. But as Paisley said, let's be sure we say that all are welcome. If we make it a Black history event, we all know what can happen."

Images of White dudes with tiki torches came to mind. Charlottesville was too close, and the events of that day were still too recent to be anything I wanted to encounter, especially at my house. "All right, so who wants to make invitations?" I said, taking Horatio's place in front of the whiteboard.

By the time everyone left around four, we had divvied out the tasks involved in preparing for the event, and I was very excited about it, even though, as Dad had cautioned, my yard was probably going to be a mess afterward. He'd know since he'd been the cause of many a mess in my yard since we'd lived here.

As we waited for the frozen chicken potpie that Horatio had brought for us to have for dinner, Santi said, "You'll be too tired to cook, I know. Consider it our way of thanking you. You do realize that our wedding is in two weeks. Here. Potentially now in the mud."

I had realized this, as I was sure he had when we talked about the event for next weekend, but I didn't care. "This is important, and honestly, if we have to deal with a little mud for our wedding, that's a small price to pay in reparation for the damage done by slavery. Plus, it's kind of fitting that we'll have a visual reminder of that history on our wedding day, isn't it?"

Santi kissed my forehead. "I knew you wouldn't be worked up about this, and I have another idea."

I looked over at him in his rocking chair and raised my eyebrows. "What's that, Mr. Shifflett?"

"What if we asked Isaiah and Mary to write and read a few words about their ancestor's history here at the start of our ceremony?" he asked.

I grinned. "I love that idea, and then we could have a moment of silence to thank those people for giving us this place."

"Beautiful," he said. "We were going to do the ceremony in the front yard, but what if we did it out back? To honor the people who were enslaved here? To be in their space, so to speak?"

"Excellent. I'll let Mika and Lucille know since they're coordinating tables and such," I said.

"And speaking of which, I asked Horatio if we could ask the tent rental company about keeping the tent up for another week after our event. I told him we'd pay for it, of course—"

"But he refused to let us, didn't he?" I asked.

Santi nodded. "I insisted, but he said absolutely not. Said it would be his wedding gift to us."

"Of course he did," I said with a laugh. "That's very kind of him, and it will make things simpler if we just have everything back there." For the next little while, he and I talked through the ceremony and the placement of things, given our new focus, and by the time I'd typed everything into a long text to Mika and Lucille, I was exhausted.

"How does going to bed, listening to the *You're Wrong About* podcast, and drifting to sleep really early sound?" I asked him.

"Sounds perfect to me," he said. "Your dad wants to get started on painting the office tomorrow at six thirty in the morning."

"Oh, glory," I said. "Thank you." I kissed him softly. "I don't know how I got so lucky."

"I ask myself the same question every day," Santi said. "Now, let's embrace middle age by eating in front of the TV and going to bed before eight p.m."

"I love you," I whispered as I went to get our dinner.

8

Santi was already outside with my dad the next morning before my brain had even begun to function, and bless my dad, he had his car radio on, playing John Denver. At one time, I loved John Denver. It was the soundtrack of my childhood. Now, as much as I appreciated the man's voice, I gritted my teeth every time I heard "Country Roads."

The song almost made a comeback for me, though, when I heard both Dad and Santi belting it out at the top of their lungs. I snuck out the backdoor and watched them. Santi was painting the trim, and Dad used the roller as they rocked out to John Denver. It might have been the cutest thing ever, and I might have videotaped it. Maybe.

When I snuck back inside to have my breakfast and, most importantly, my coffee, Mika texted. "Did you see the numbers from the City Market yesterday?"

"I haven't gotten to my email yet. How'd we do?"

"Double our normal," she replied.

That had me scrambling for my laptop, and sure enough, Randy had emailed his figures for the day. I didn't know if it was him, what we'd had to sell, or just a stellar day, but we had almost grossed double our usual. It was amazing.

"Wow," I texted back. "Want to come over and celebrate by watching that movie *Kate* with me?"

"I'll be over in an hour," she said.

I felt kind of bad leaving my dad and Santi to do the work, but I knew I needed to rest, especially with what was coming up for the next two weeks. Santi needed rest, too, but hopefully, he'd be able to get some downtime at work. That sounded paradoxical, but as he often told me, a lot of his job was simply to be available. And sometimes, being *available* meant napping with his phone nearby.

After I ate my Raisin Bran and had my second cup of coffee, I went out to see how the guys were progressing. It turned out they were almost done with the primer. "Wow," I said. "You made fast work of this!"

"It's a ten-by-twelve space, Pais," Dad said. "It would have been fast with just a paintbrush."

Santi touched the back wall. "And given the hot, dry air, it's almost ready for that macaroni and cheese color you picked out."

"You're kidding, right?" Dad said. "You aren't painting the walls that neon orange."

"Not the color of boxed mac and cheese. More a golden yellow. I wanted a sunny space to work," I said as I grabbed the paint can and showed him the spot on the lid. "It'll be lovely."

"Plus, you'll hardly see it under all the things your daughter is planning to hang in here," Santi said with a smirk.

I smacked his arm, but he wasn't wrong. I did have a lot of my favorite salvaged items that I wanted to use to decorate. I couldn't wait.

"Mika is coming over to watch a movie in a bit. Need us to help?" I asked. I knew what their answer would be, but again, I needed to ask for Dad's sake.

"Nope, honey, you go rest," Dad said. "We'll be done by noon."

I didn't have to be told twice. I kissed Santi on the cheek and hugged my dad before trotting back inside to make Mika and me some mimosas and set up our viewing station. Both she and I were of the opinion that watching TV properly involved blankets, so I kicked up the AC and pulled the two comfiest quilts I owned out of the trunk. Then I set up a tray table with our drinks and snacks—Sunchips and dark chocolate. When she arrived, we hugged, then sat down. This was about companionship, not chatting, and both of us were fine with that fact.

By the time the movie was over, we were draped over each other and completely relaxed. I could have taken a nap that way and had on many occasions, but now I was actually eager to talk. "So the market was amazing yesterday, huh?" I said as I picked up our glasses and carried them to the kitchen. "Did you have something special there?"

Mika shook her head as she put the tray table away. "Nope. Just my usual. You?"

"Nothing out of the ordinary. I did send over a floating mantel, but that was only a couple of hundred dollars," I said. "Did you look at the numbers?"

"Not yet," she said. "Want to do it together?"

I grabbed my laptop and popped open the point-of-sale software so that we could take a look. "Okay, here we go," I said as Mika slid her chair next to mine at the dining room table.

We scanned the sales figures from the day before for a few seconds, and for the most part, the day was pretty normal. A few sales of weird little tchotchkes we'd found or made—including a rabbit finial I'd had for almost a year and was delighted to see it had found a home. When we got to the end of the records, though, there it was, the source of our banner day—someone had bought not only the floating mantel I'd sent on a whim but also four window frames and two candelabras. It was a single sale of over a thousand dollars, the uppermost end of what we normally made on a very good fair day.

"Look at their credit card. Who bought all of that?" Mika said.

I flipped over to the name from the card and studied it for a minute. "Davis Mackey," it read.

"That can't be a coincidence," I said to Mika. "Right?"

"No way," she agreed. "Do we know who he is?"

"Not yet," I said and opened up a search tab. A couple of taps later, we had a man named Joel Mackey living in Barboursville. "That can't be a coincidence."

"Looks like we're going back into their papers," Mika said as she stood up. "We need more mimosas."

Even with all our work the previous two days, we hadn't made it through all the Mackey papers. Given that we'd identified Isaiah LeVarge definitely and had plans to find out more about his family the following Saturday, the Mackeys had been sort of shunted to the side.

Now, though, I had a reason to go back in. "Let's start with the most recent stuff since this man is alive," I suggested.

"Good plan," Mika said as she set two more glasses of orange juice and champagne on the counter. "Drink up, and I'll get the tote out." She took a long sip of her drink—fortification, I suppose—and headed into the living room.

I sipped from my glass a bit more slowly as I thought about what we needed to look up. First, I realized that I didn't know Ms. Mackey's first name, and while she hadn't said she had a partner, I wanted to check into that. It was likely that she was born with the name Mackey, given her investment in the family story, but I had known a lot of people who married into families and took up the mantle for their history more than the people who had been raised in the family.

Then I wanted to see how Davis Mackey was related to Ms.

Mackey before we searched to figure out how they were related to Joel.

I made notes with those goals on a slip of paper as I sat down next to Mika on the couch with Beauregard stretched out to the size of a small giraffe between us and took the folder she handed me.

"I'll work from the front," she said. "You go from the back."

I nodded and opened the most recent collection of records, which looked to be mostly newspaper clippings from the early 2000s but nothing from the last fifteen years or so. That made sense since many folks didn't get the newspaper anymore and read it online instead. I made a note to do an online newspaper search when we were done with the paper.

But even without anything from the last decade in the files, I did find Davis Mackey in one article. Apparently, in eighth grade at Octonia Middle, he won a debate contest. I showed Mika the article and then did some quick math. If he was four-teen in eighth grade, then he was probably born around 1990. I made a note and kept searching.

It took me four folders before I found Ms. Mackey's first name, Olivia, in a newspaper article about a holiday bazaar back in 1989. She had apparently been selling hand-woven shawls, and there was a picture of her with a beautiful piece of yarn work. Remarkably, she looked the same, but her face was less stern in the photo than it was now. It didn't look like life had been easy for her over the past thirty years. But then, it hadn't been easy on most of us, I suppose.

I passed the article over to Mika, and as she read it, Santi came in. "Your dad and I have some errands to run." He winked at me. "See you in a couple of hours. I'll pick up Saw on the way back if that works."

My fiancé didn't just "run errands," and my dad actively avoided them. But I already had one mystery to solve, so I didn't push. "That would be great. His dad is expecting us at five."

"I'm on it," he said as he kissed my cheek and went out the door.

"What was that about?" Mika asked.

I shook my head. "Got no idea, but I am curious." I glanced down at the article still in her hand. "She's got some yarn skills, doesn't she?"

"She does. And I think this yarn might have been hand-made, too. Hard to tell from the photo, but it looks it." She pulled the photo up closer to her eyes and studied it. "Did you see any looms or anything at her house when you were there?"

"Nope," I said, "but I have an idea. Mary and Isaiah are doing some investigation after church today, so why don't we do the same? Let's go see Olivia Mackey," I said. "If we finish up this tote, we can take all but the first one back to her as a reason for our visit."

"Good plan," she said. "But no more mimosas for me then. I need to at least appear sensible when we go visiting." She laughed and went back to her folder.

The rest of that tote yielded a bunch of family anecdotes but nothing related to the LeVarges. We packed everything up quickly and loaded the three totes into the car.

"What are you going to tell her about the first one?" Mika asked as we pulled up the driveway. "You're not going to tell her Xzanthia has it, are you?"

"Absolutely not," I said. "I'm just going to say that I was fascinated by the broader historical information her family history revealed about Octonia and that I was using that early history to fashion an article."

"So you're going to write an article about them just to avoid lying?" Mika said with a laugh.

"Precisely," I said. "First, I have to do the one about Isaiah LeVarge, but then I'll write up the Mackeys story for the following week." Hopefully, by then, we'd have more information connecting the two families, and the articles would make a good complementary pair.

Ms. Mackey was waiting on the front porch of her house when we arrived, and she smiled at us warmly as we pulled the totes out from the back of my car. "My driveway alarm went off, and I was thrilled to see it was you." She pointed toward the boxes. "Were the papers helpful?"

"Oh yes, ma'am," I said as we carried two of them to the porch, and Mika went back for the third. "In fact, I kept one of them—I hope that's okay—because I want to write an article about the early history of your family here in Octonia. Would that be all right?"

A flush of pink came into her cheeks, and her smile widened. "That would be lovely. I'm sure you'll do a wonderful job, and if you need me to look it over before you publish it, just let me know." Her voice was casual, but I heard the request in it.

I hated committing to having a pre-publication review, but I also didn't want to put her off. "I'll keep that in mind," I said as Mika came up with the final box. "This is my friend, Mika. She owns the yarn store in town."

Mika smiled. "I saw a newspaper article about your shawls. Do you still knit?"

"Weave, actually, but yes. Do you?" Ms. Mackey asked as she opened the front door for us.

"I don't, but I'd love to learn. I was actually hoping to offer a weaving class this fall. Maybe you'd teach it for us?" Mika winked at me as she followed Ms. Mackey into the living room.

Ms. Mackey smiled and said, "Well, I would be delighted. Would you like to see my setup?"

"Oh yes," Mika said with genuine delight.

"I'll get the other two boxes and put them in the living room," I said as the two women went through the back door of the library.

Mika squealed a few seconds later, and I knew I had lost her to yarn for at least the next little bit.

With the totes put back where Ms. Mackey had found them, I decided to explore the room. As our hostess had hinted, the books were quite old, and I couldn't resist running my fingers over the spines. I didn't recognize most of the titles or authors since these books seemed to be largely about agriculture and science, but they were so beautiful.

Eventually, I made my way to the back of the room and followed the women's voices to find them in a wonderfully sunny atrium where two gigantic looms were set up. Ms. Mackey was sitting at one of them, working on something made from purple and blue yarn with silver feathered through. It was beautiful. "That looks like the night sky," I said.

Ms. Mackey looked up from her work and laughed. "What a lovely description. I think that's what I'll call it." She did one more pedal on the machine and then pointed Mika toward a series of low shelves sitting beneath the windows circling the room. "I've been very fortunate to have my own sheep and alpacas, and my nephew helps me care for them and shear when it's time. So I make my own yarn."

"I thought so," Mika said. "May I?" She stretched out her fingers toward a bin of beautiful pink and orange yarn.

"Of course. Yarn is meant to be touched," Ms. Mackey said.

I couldn't resist either and went and stuck my hand in a bin of what must have been alpaca yarn because it was so soft. "This is amazing."

"You must let me make you something from that, then," Ms. Mackey said. "As a thank you."

"I would love to have one of your pieces, but I want to pay for it." I kept my voice firm. This woman did amazing work, and she deserved compensation. Too many of us gave our work away for free, and I wasn't going to be a part of that.

Ms. Mackey blushed. "Well, then, I'd be honored to have you pay for it."

"Actually, do you want to sell some of your things in my store? Your yarn and also your finished products?" Mika asked.

Ms. Mackey looked away and took a deep breath. When she answered, her voice sounded tight. "I would love that. Can I stop by tomorrow and bring you some things to consider?"

"Perfect," Mika said. "We can get the date and details set for your weaving class then, too."

"Oh, maybe I'll weave your scarf during the class, Paisley," she said in a high-pitched voice.

"Great idea," I said and looked over at Mika.

"Actually, Ms. Mackey," she smiled at the older woman. "May I call you Olivia?"

"Ollie, if you will," Ollie said. "It's what all my friends call me."

"Ollie," Mika said with a smile, "we actually had a couple of questions for you about your family if you have time."

"And I wanted to share what we found, too, so that you can add it to your files," I said.

Ollie's smile faded a bit, but she led us back to the library. "Can I get you some tea?" she asked.

"Do you have it iced and sweet?" I asked.

"Is there any other way?" Ollie said. "I'll be right back."

While she got our tea, Mika and I gathered our questions and decided I would begin by telling her what we knew about Joel Mackey and his land. I was definitely going to share that he had enslaved at least four people, but I also wanted to be sure she knew that while that fact was horrible, it was still typical for that time period. Her shame about her family's history would get in the way of any healing that could come for her or others, so any way that we could alleviate that would be helpful.

When Ollie returned with three tall glasses of sweet tea, she set them on a small coffee table and took her seat in a chair several feet away. I took a deep breath. She clearly wasn't very eager for this conversation.

"Ollie," I said, "we did find your ancestor Joel's land records. You may know some of this, so please stop me if I'm giving you some information you don't need." I told her about when her ancestor bought his land and built his house. I also told her about his enslaved labor but went on to say that he worked alongside them. "He was a mason and learned his trade from an enslaved man named Peyton Skipwith. Since we know Peyton worked to build many of the buildings at UVA, we think Joel might have done the same."

This last bit of information seemed to perk our host up a bit. "I went to UVA, so I might have been in buildings my ancestor built."

"That's very well possible. If we find out more specifics about Joel's work, we'll certainly let you know." I looked out the window to the field in front of the house before continuing. "I also want you to know that one of the men Joel enslaved and who worked for him after slavery ended was murdered and buried on the property I now own."

Ollie gasped and put a hand to her mouth. "No, how terrible."

I nodded. "The man's name was Isaiah LeVarge, and he was also a mason, probably trained by your ancestor. We don't know the details of his death yet, but it's likely going to be part of the news around town for a bit. So I wanted you to know."

She studied my face for a long minute before saying, "Did Joel have anything to do with it?"

As hard as the possibility must have been to consider, I admired Ollie for being willing to know that it was a possibility. "We don't know yet," I said. "The account we have is from Isaiah's son, and he reports two men killed his dad. But nothing else."

"Do my records shed any light?" she said. "I'd hate to hear

that my ancestor was involved, but it's worse not to know who killed someone." Once again, she seemed to be holding back tears.

This woman was quite a different figure than the angry person shouting at Xzanthia. I wasn't sure what to make of that. "Not as of yet," I said. "But would you like me to let you know if we find anything there?"

She nodded. "Yes, but also do tell the sheriff. I would never want to stand in the way of justice."

Mika shot me a quick glance out of the corner of her eye, but I nodded. I was baffled by Ollie's reaction, too, but then again, people often surprised me.

"I will do that, Ollie," I said, then patted my knees and stood up. "Thank you for having us, and I will get that last box of records back to you as soon as possible." I stepped forward and put out my arms, hoping it was okay to want to hug her.

Apparently, it was since she squeezed me so tightly that I heard my spine crack.

Mika also gave the woman a hug and then said, "I'll see you tomorrow at the shop so we can get planning and selling some of your things."

"I look forward to it," she said. "Thank you."

"No, thank you," I said with a smile and then, before I could think better of it, I quickly said, "Ollie, we're also having a genealogy day at my house on Saturday. We're mostly trying to find out more about Isaiah LeVarge's family and the families of the other people who were enslaved on my property. But anyone is welcome, and I'd love it if you were there."

Ollie looked at me carefully. "Thank you for that kind invitation. May I think about it?"

"Of course," I said. "Just come if you decide you'd like to. We'll start at eleven a.m." I hugged her again quickly, and then we slipped back out the front door.

As we got into the car, Mika said, "That was a pretty big change of heart, wasn't it?"

I nodded. My brain was trying to tell me to be skeptical, to doubt her sincerity, but I was learning to trust my heart, and it was telling me to accept the gift of a changed heart. I decided to go with it.

9

The next few days were a whirlwind of activities, both to prepare for the genealogy event and with wedding prep. We'd gotten most of our wedding plans secured weeks ago, but small things just kept coming up, like Sawyer's refusal to wear a bowtie. He had decided he wanted to wear a tie like the one his Boppi did, and while I didn't care much in terms of aesthetics, we had already ordered him a bowtie to go with the brown linen suit we'd bought him.

Fortunately, Lucille said she'd take care of changing the order when I was listing off my to-dos on Wednesday morning. "That, I can do. But I cannot help you with pricing corbels. I have no idea how you know what to charge for those things," she said as she loaded Sawyer into the car for the trip to school.

"I wing it mostly," I said. "I guess I could try to be competitive, but if I can make a little off each sale, I figure that's good enough." *Especially with the other big sales we've had this month*, I thought to myself. I didn't talk about finances very often with my parents, only because my dad worried so much that I wasn't okay. I was okay, though. Better than okay, but I didn't think there was any figure I could give him that would assure him of that fact. So I didn't even try.

Just now, though, Dad was on my mind for other reasons, namely that I had been forbidden to enter my own office because he and Santi were doing something in there. They'd even covered the new French doors in craft paper, but I knew furniture was involved since I could hear scooting. I had visions of some formal office set or something made from pressed particle board. Like I needed one more thing to worry about just now.

I wandered back to my office and shouted through the door. "I'm heading out, Dad. Make yourself at home." He'd been there since seven doing whatever he was doing, and I knew he was due for breakfast soon. "Bacon and coffee are in the kitchen."

"Thank you. Now go on, honey. I'm just fine." I heard him harumph behind the door, but I didn't even ask.

"See you later," I shouted and went to my car. Claire had just bought a bunch of new items, including a variety of corbels, and she wanted my help in pricing them. The woman was capable of doing this herself, but I knew what it felt like to feel insecure about a new role, so I was happy to help.

When I arrived, she was at the desk with a variety of items around her, and she looked absolutely lost. "Oh, hi," she said. "We have a customer already."

I looked down at my watch, and it was only eight forty-five. We didn't technically open until ten. "Oh?" I said.

"I told him about our hours, but he asked if he could please come in since he planned to make a large purchase." Claire looked at me with concern.

I came around the desk and hugged her. "You made the right call. Are these the things we're holding while he shops?" I asked as I studied the items on the desk.

She nodded and then looked over at the stairs as heavy footfalls sounded on them. "Here he comes," she whispered.

A tall, lean man with light brown skin came toward us and set down two iron candle sconces. "I just have one more room to go through, and then I think I'll be set for today." He smiled at me and then looked back at Claire. "You have the best things. I bought a bunch of stuff at your stall on Saturday and had to come to the flagship store itself."

Before I thought about it, I blurted, "You're Davis Mackey."

When the man stared at me, I thought to put out my hand. "I'm Paisley Sutton, the shop owner, and this is Claire, our stellar soon-to-be store manager."

Claire blinked and then smiled at me before turning back to Mackey. "You were at our stall?"

Mackey looked at her and then at me before shaking my hand. "I was, but unless you are psychic, I'm not sure how you know my name."

I laughed. "I am indeed psychic, and I can read credit card charges. We were so wowed by your big purchase that I had to know who you were."

"Ah, that explains it," Mackey said. "I had been hoping to go incognito, but my spy skills aren't up to par. Next time, I'll use cash." He smiled, but he still didn't look thrilled.

I cleared my throat. "Don't worry. We aren't spreading the word about your purchases or anything. We take confidentiality very seriously." I suddenly felt nervous that I had offended the man.

His smile got bigger. "Oh, it's not that. I just didn't want my aunt to know. She's a proud woman, and I don't want her thinking I'm trying to compensate for something she didn't do."

A bing of recognition went off in my head, but I decided to keep my mouth shut. "I'm not sure I understand."

Mackey smiled again. "You've actually met my aunt. In fact, I think you were at her house on Sunday. Olivia Mackey, Ollie."

I clapped my hands. "You're Ollie's nephew? Wow. Small world."

"Sort of. When I saw your stall at the market, I wanted to support you since you've given my aunt something to think about besides her decaying house for the past few days. She was very excited that you were interested in our family history," Davis said. "She's an amazing woman but too humble for her own good."

I walked out from behind the counter. "I know, right? I saw her weaving when we were there. Gorgeous. More people need to know about what she does."

"Well, as I understand it, your friend Mika is taking care of that," Davis said as he picked up a lamp made from old power-line insulators and carried it over to where Claire stood with a look of surprise on her face. She'd been trying to sell that hideous lamp for months.

"We try to support our community," I said. "And honestly, Mika was so excited to have her yarn and scarves in the shop. I think she's already sold some."

"How about that?" Davis said. "Maybe Aunt Ollie will be able to actually do some of the repairs to the house that she's been talking about."

I nodded. "I noticed the house needed a little work, but I know those places can be real money pits." I gestured around my store. "That's why I'm in business. A lot of people just can't afford to keep the houses intact, which is a real shame."

"It is, and I wish Aunt Ollie would let me help, but she just can't. The best I can do is help her with her animals," Davis said.

"Oh, you're the nephew who cares for the alpacas and goats. That's nice of you," I said.

"Actually, I love it." He looked back at the stairs. "I better finish my shopping. I'm donating some of these things to the silent auction at the firehouse during the holidays. Mind if I mention you?"

I shook my head. "And get me the details. I'll donate a couple of larger items, too," I said. "Forgive my skepticism, but do you think corbels will go at a silent auction?"

"Oh no," he said. "Those are for Aunt Ollie's house. I'm going to tell her I just came upon them. They're a lot like the ones on the front porch, and I figure if I tell her I'd like to keep them from going to the landfill, I can probably fix her porch at the same time."

"Good plan," I said. This guy was a good one. Ollie was lucky to have him. "Hey, before you go, I don't know what Ollie has told you about the research I'm doing, but if you're free and interested, we're having a little research day at my house on Saturday. I invited your aunt, and you are welcome to come."

Davis shook his head. "She didn't mention it, but she loves history. I'll see if I can't get her to come along.

He headed upstairs, and I looked over at Claire. "Give him a good deal on those corbels," I said quietly. "Cost, okay?"

"You got it," Claire said. "And now I don't need you anymore. Your work here is done."

I looked at the stairwell. "I suppose it is. I suppose it is."

IT WAS when I was back in my car and heading toward Mika's shop to work for a bit before grabbing an early lunch that I realized I hadn't asked Davis Mackey what he did for a living. For a man who appeared to be in his early thirties, he seemed to have some cash and some time. His clothes—business casual of the highest end—made me think he might have an office job, but then, he knew how to shear goats and alpacas. He was a mystery, for sure.

At Mika's shop, I sat down and went to work on the newsletter about the LeVarges. Xzanthia had written up a time line of all the Isaiahs and had provided me with their spouses and children where possible. But how Isaiah II had been trained as a mason by Skipwith was the real start of my story, and the end was going to be his murder.

When I'd talked to Xzanthia the day before, she hadn't been able to find anything further about the murder in the Mackey's papers, which was both disappointing and relieving, but her digging had turned up a small newspaper account from Charlottesville's Black newspaper that basically gave the same fact as Isaiah III's church announcement. Except for one thing—the newspaper said the men were White.

That crucial fact was neither surprising nor incidental, especially when paired with what Mary and Isaiah had been able to learn from the elders at their church. It turned out that Isaiah II's murder had been, unsurprisingly, a bit of a story in their parents' time, big enough that it was passed down. The oral history was that Isaiah had purportedly been found reading a novel, *Oliver Twist,* at the train station.

"Folks didn't like that much," Mary had told me on Monday when we'd met for coffee. "The men who found him gave him a good beating that day and took his book." Mary rolled her eyes. "The irony was that Isaiah didn't think those men could read at all. They were just threatened that he could."

I sighed. There really was nothing to say about that kind of racism and ignorance.

"Did anyone have any sense of who did it?" I finally asked.

Mary shook her head. "Nope. They told us that if their parents had known, they probably wouldn't have said since knowing might have put the kids in danger." She took a sip of her iced coffee. "I totally understand that, but from where we sit now, it's frustrating."

After I finished chewing my bite of croissant, I agreed. "It used to be that I hated all kinds of secrets, that I thought they denoted shame or ugliness that people should just own or out."

I looked at my friend and said, "But now I know it's a privilege not to have to keep secrets. One more thing my white skin gives me."

Mary smiled and put her hand on mine. "You know, woman, I'm so glad you teach yourself, and I don't have to."

I laughed at that, even though there was a weight to the statement that wasn't at all funny. "Well, that gives us a bit more to go on, I guess, but it still doesn't get us much closer to knowing who killed Isaiah II."

"No, it doesn't," she agreed. "But while I think it's probably an exercise in complete futility, I'm going to head to the clerk's office and see if there might be anything in the court records. It's a total long shot, but we have to take all our shots, huh?"

"We do," I said. "Let me know if you find anything?"

IN MY ARTICLE, I was going to be sure to mention the story about the book and say it was possibly a motive for murder. If nothing else, the story might drive home the depth of racism during that time, and if we were lucky, it might cause some folks to pull up short and look at their own prejudices now. I knew a fair number of White folks who still assumed Black folks were uneducated and unintelligent.

I wrote up the rest of the article and ended with, "If you know anything about the murder of Isaiah LeVarge in roughly 1870-1880, the family would be grateful to hear it. Thank you." I included my email address for easy reference and then scheduled the message to send to my two thousand or so subscribers in an hour.

With that work done, I wandered over to where Mika and Mrs. Stephenson were sorting a huge basket of gorgeous yarn I recognized. "Is that all from Ollie?" I said.

"Yep," Mika answered. "She's got quite a stash. All hand-made." She passed me a hank of the softest baby-pink yarn I'd ever felt.

"Wow. I love this, and while I'm not really a pink-loving woman, I would take a scarf in this anytime," I said.

"I was thinking a toboggan myself," Mrs. Stephenson said.

"Oh, good idea," I replied, imagining the soft texture around my ears. "Who wants to make it for me?" I said with a laugh.

Mika tugged the yarn from my hand and made a note in her ledger. "Consider it your Christmas present."

"Excellent," I said. "So you bought everything?"

"I tried, but she insisted on doing it on consignment," Mika said. "Fortunately, we've already sold all of that." She pointed to a small stack in the corner of the counter behind the register.

"It's too lovely to pass up," Mrs. Stephenson said with a glint in her eye. "I'll make everyone mittens this year."

Mrs. Stephenson had become Mika's right-hand woman in the past couple of years, and she and I were good friends now, too. She was always there when we needed help, and she'd quite literally saved me several times.

"I like how you think," I said. "I'll mention to Lucille that she might need to stock up, too."

As we all continued to sort the yarn into rough color groups, Mrs. Stephenson said, "So, an interesting thing happened yesterday."

Mika and I both looked at her and then went back to sorting. "Yeah?" Mika said.

"Well, while you two were out at the final fitting for your dress," Mrs. Stephenson winked at me, "a man came in. Tall, dark, and handsome for sure. Said he was looking to buy some hand-spun yarn."

"A man came in?" I asked. Men shoppers in Mika's store were pretty rare.

"And he knew to ask for home-spun yarn?" Mika asked before shaking her head. "Sorry, we're stereotyping. Go on."

"Well, I was surprised, too, but I pointed him to the skeins of Ollie's yarn that we had already put out. He bought them all." She looked at Mika. "Every single one."

I scowled. "Did this man pay with a credit card?"

Mrs. Stephenson said and looked at me. "Odd you say that because he mentioned that he'd learned to pay with cash since word travels if he doesn't."

"Definitely Davis Mackey," I said with a smile. "He's trying to support his Aunt Ollie without her knowing it. He bought a ton of stuff from me this morning and said he was going to donate some for a silent auction and then convince Ollie to use some of it on her house."

"Why do I suddenly feel like we're on the ethical version of *Ozark* right now?" Mika said.

"Only if I get to be Laura Linney," I replied. "Seems like a good guy. Did he say anything about himself?"

"Yeah, like, is he single?" Mika asked. Her last relationship with a good friend of Santi's had ended a few months before, amicably but still painfully. It had taken a while, but she was back on the market, at least casually.

Mrs. Stephenson shook her head. "I don't know his marital status, although he didn't wear a wedding ring," she said as she hip-bumped Mika. "I got you, girl."

I laughed. "Any chance he mentioned what he did for a living?" I asked. "I'm just being nosy," I admitted.

Mrs. Stephenson chuckled. "Actually, he runs an internet marketing company. We got talking about being business owners, and it just came up. I take it from what he said that the company is quite successful."

I smiled and nodded. Mrs. Stephenson was a very discreet woman when it came to finances. Her accounting career had made that innate, but for the same reason, she was very good at evaluating someone's financial status. If she said someone's business was successful, it was successful. And that explained how Davis could afford to buy a ton of yarn *and* a ton of salvaged goods.

"Seems like you're both having a great month," she said. "Between Horatio Denver and Davis Mackey, your revenues are going to be amazing." Since Mrs. Stephenson was the book-keeper and accountant for both our businesses, I knew she took some personal joy in that. "More work for me is a good thing," she said.

I laughed. "I'm glad to hear it." With a glance at Mika, I said, "I'm starving, and I really need my maid of honor to help me with some last-minute details. Are you ready?"

"For the bride, anything," Mika said. "Be back in an hour," she told Mrs. Stephenson.

"I've got the store," Mrs. Stephenson said. "You never know. I might just sell out of yarn while you're gone."

The three of us laughed as Mika and I grabbed our things and headed to the inn for burgers. Some brides might have been starving themselves before their wedding, but I was going into that amazing day with a full stomach and a light heart. Santi loved me as I was, and I was learning to do the same. And self-love today looked like a bacon cheeseburger at the best burger place around.

10

Thursday morning came very early with a nudge from Beauregard on my nose. Apparently, he was dissatisfied with his sleeping position directly against my face and wanted my entire pillow for himself instead.

Normally, I'd just jettison him from the bed and go back to sleep, but given all that was happening with the genealogy day and our wedding, I was in a season of if I was awakened, I was really awakened. It was five a.m., so I got out of bed and watched Beau spin himself into position on my pillow before I tiptoed out of the room, past Sawyer's open bedroom door, and down to the kitchen, where I made coffee and opened my laptop.

The night before, Santi and I had gone over our wedding checklist one last time and declared that everything that could be done in advance was done. The rest would have to happen next week, which left me to focus on the genealogy day on Saturday.

Mary had extended the invite to the Black churches, and while we weren't asking people to RSVP formally, we'd already heard that we could expect at least a few dozen people, including a bunch of folks who were coming with family photos for us to scan. Horatio and Isaiah had dropped the scanners by Mika's store earlier in the week, and Isaiah had just sent me the link to the website.

He'd called it Octonia's Faces, and it looked amazing. He'd uploaded some of his and Mary's family photos and written text to describe the purpose of the site. Then he had put up a basic form that let people identify the photos by number and share whatever information they might have about them. It was a basic design, and I expected even those unfamiliar with website forms would find it simple to use.

I sent him a note and told him the site looked great and attached digital copies of a couple of photos I'd found over the years for him to upload as more examples. If we did this right, I expected this site would quickly become very popular. I hoped Isaiah was ready for a deluge of photos and information.

My next email took some of the joy out of me, though, because Xzanthia had written around midnight asking if I could come in as early as possible that morning. "I found the information we've been seeking, and we need to make a plan," she said.

My stomach dropped to my knees. This was the information we had been hoping for, but it was surely going to be a bombshell for our community if Xzanthia said we needed to have a plan.

I took a deep breath and wrote her back. "I'll be in as soon as I get Sawyer to school. I'll ask Santi to come, too."

Her response was almost immediate. "Good. See you then." She must have been up all night, another harbinger that things were not great in the world of history.

By some grace, Sawyer was actually easygoing that morning and not only got dressed immediately but asked to eat Raisin Bran for breakfast. We were out the door with almost no battle, and that simple reality made me feel ready to take on the world.

That was until I walked into the historical society a half-hour later and saw the look on Xzanthia's face, her face ashen with dark circles under her eyes, and while her makeup and hair were as flawless as usual, she looked exhausted. I was glad I had brought her a coffee, although I felt like maybe I should have picked up a cot on the way over.

"You all right?" I said. "Long night?"

She nodded. "Very," she said. "But productive. You know how it goes. I got on the trail of a lead, and I couldn't let it go."

"I absolutely understand." I put the large cup of coffee in front of her. "No sugar, triple cream," I said.

"Bless you." She picked up the cup and took a long drink. "All right, you better sit down."

I did as she suggested and said, "That bad, huh?"

"Woman, you have no idea. Brace yourself."

I considered gripping the side of the table, but I settled for holding my coffee mug more tightly. "All right, I'm ready. What did you find?"

"Well, let's begin with what we knew—Isaiah III's account of what happened to his father." She pulled out the newspaper article Horatio had read to us at our house. "So, that's the first thing I started researching—the old church."

"Right, and you found it, I take it?" I asked.

"I did," she said and slid an old photograph toward me. "This is Zion AME Church. It burned down in 1925, and because the congregation was so small at the time of the fire, they didn't rebuild." She passed over another newspaper article that talked about the fire and then another that noted the members were simply going to join other churches.

"That seems rare to me that a church wouldn't rebuild. A lot of congregations around here are holding on with just a few members, but they don't shutter their doors." I looked up from the article, and Xzanthia was nodding.

"That was my impression, too, so I did a bit more digging." She passed over a photocopy of some handwritten pages. "The article about the fire quotes Ms. Harriet Venture. That name sounded familiar to me, and sure enough, when I looked into our files, I found that her family had donated her papers. These are pages from her journal."

I read them to myself, and then as the action in the journal got more intense, I began to read aloud. "We'd known this day could come, that they might decide to try to shut us up at some point, but we hadn't thought they'd be so bold as to set fire to the church on a Sunday morning when we were in worship."

I stared at the page for a long moment and then looked at Xzanthia. "Someone tried to burn the church down when it was full of people?"

"Keep reading," she said.

"The fire began simultaneously at all the doors to the church—the main one and the two at the front through which the choir members usually entered. It spread quickly because the building was so old, and if it hadn't been for the quick thinking of two young men who grabbed the pastor's chair from the altar and threw it through one of the stained glass windows, we would have all died."

"Holy cow," I said.

Xzanthia nodded and then looked back at the pages.

I read on. "We should have long ago turned in the men who killed Isaiah some fifty years ago. Lord knows, I thought about it many a time, especially when the threats started appearing after his son began to lose his good sense and talked about these things at the bar on a Friday night. But I suppose we all thought it would blow over, that Isaiah would eventually lose his mind enough to drink that he couldn't talk at all. We were wrong."

I put down the pages and stared at my friend. "Someone burned down the church because Isaiah III was talking about who killed his father." The weight of knowledge sat like lead in my stomach.

"Yes. So I dug further." She pulled a very old, stained book out from the stack next to her and passed it my way. "Take a look at the page I marked," she said.

I flipped the book open to her bookmark and saw it was a series of scrawling notes written in a bunch of different people's handwriting. I scanned a few and then asked, "Okay, I have no idea. What is it?"

"It's a tavern journal from the Two Nickels."

"The dive bar just over there?" I pointed up Main Street to where the seedy bar sat a block down a side street. It had a reputation for being the place to go if you wanted to be over-served and ignored. I had been once when I was in high school because they never carded anyone, but then, it was mostly for the thrill of visiting the place. I had been creeped out by the whole event and never went back.

"Same one. It's an Octonia landmark, and a few years ago, the current owners gave us a set of journals that have apparently been a facet of the culture there for almost a hundred years." She tapped the book in front of me with a long fingernail. "This is the journal that covers the years 1925-1929."

I looked back down at the jagged handwriting on the pages and nodded. "So patrons just jotted down entries when they felt like it? Like a guest book?"

"More like the diary for the bar," Xzanthia said. "Read here." She pointed to a particularly long entry at the bottom of the page she had marked.

"I have to get this off my chest finally. I've known he killed my daddy for decades now, and it's been eating me from the inside out. Sylvester Mackey and Donald Robinson murdered my father. People have been saying it was because he was reading or some such nonsense. Nope, they killed him for his money. Same as most folks get killed for. Killed him, took the cash out of his pockets, and then came here to drink it away. I've kept this secret too long, and now, now this book can keep it for me. – I 3."

"Isaiah the third," I said as I ran my fingers over his handwriting. "He expunged the secret from himself, but why do it here? Why in this book?"

"That was my question, too, and it turns out he probably had some sort of dementia, maybe brought on by too much drinking. The secondary cause of death was cirrhosis of the liver." She pulled up his death certificate on her computer, and his primary cause of death was pneumonia caused by aspiration of food.

"He got pneumonia because he couldn't eat properly. So dementia inadvertently caused his death," I said.

Xzanthia nodded again. "That's how I understand that, too. So I looked into Sylvester Mackey and Donald Robinson."

"Mackey is related to Ollie and Davis, I expect."

"Yep," she said. "He's Ollie's great uncle, and he did have a reputation for being kind of a hooligan. Robinson, too. They show up in the police blotter for a lot of arrests related to vandalism, harassment, that kind of thing."

"But not murder?" I asked.

"Nope, nothing that serious that I can find. But then, if they were just killing Black people . . ." She grew quiet.

"It's possible no one ever investigated those deaths." I groaned. "This just keeps getting more awful."

"What keeps getting more awful?" Santi said from the doorway. He'd had to stop by work before coming over, but I was glad he was here now.

Xzanthia showed him what she had found, and when she was done, she said, "I hope that helps you close the case, Sheriff."

Santi stared down at the journal and then looked up at Xzanthia. "You've done a lot of good work here. Thank you. I'll definitely follow up on everything as best I can."

I studied his face for a moment. "But?"

"But this isn't firm enough evidence to close the case. It's hearsay from a man who was suffering from both an addiction and a serious mental health condition. I need more to be able to say definitively that the killers were Mackey and Robinson." He shook his head. "I'm so sorry. I think we'd all like to have some answers here, but this isn't enough, but it's a great start."

The lines of fatigue on Xzanthia's face grew deeper, but she nodded. "I understand. I'll keep looking."

"You will," I said, "but not right now. Now you need to go home and get some sleep. All of this can wait until tomorrow."

Normally, Xzanthia Nicholas didn't let anyone tell her what to do, but either the fatigue or the discouragement was getting to her, and she just nodded. "Sounds good," she said quietly.

Santi and I helped her turn out the lights and lock the doors, and then I walked her to her car and hugged her before she left. I hoped she was just exhausted, but her melancholy seemed more intense than just the lack of sleep.

"I'll call her tomorrow," I said when I got to my car and found Santi waiting there.

"Good." He pulled me against his chest. "Sometimes I hate my job," he whispered into my hair.

"I know," I said. "Me, too." I wasn't sure if I meant I hated his job or mine, but it really didn't matter. Some days were just really hard.

FORTUNATELY, we had something to take our mind off the sadness of all this news—the tent was being set up at our house this afternoon, and I was picking Sawyer up early from school so he could see it. I had a feeling that boy would talk the tent-setters into letting him help wield a hammer, and I wouldn't be surprised if he drove one of those huge stakes right into the ground. He was a force, that little man.

We grabbed some fast food on the way home from his school, and by the time Santi, Sawyer, and I arrived home, the tent truck was there, and the crew was in the midst of pulling out the giant canvas on the field below the house. Sawyer didn't even wait for us to get out of the car before he sprinted down the hill. Within minutes, he was pulling on one corner next to a young man who was laughing and gesturing to all his crewmates as Saw tugged that massive thing flat in that area.

"I'll go down and be sure he doesn't kill himself or anyone else," Santi said with a laugh.

"Thanks," I said. "I'll get the iced tea and bring it and some plastic cups down. It's hot enough to melt even the most hardened worker today."

Santi laughed as he wandered down the hill. "Pull, Saw, pull," he shouted.

Inside, I took a couple of minutes to breathe the cool air and check on Beauregard, who was, of course, on his blanket with his nose tucked under a paw. Apparently, I had the air set a little too low for his highness.

It wasn't too low for me, and no matter how much stinkeye he gave me from over that paw, the AC was going to keep pumping. "Get under your blanket, Beau. You'll be fine." He closed his eyes in what I took to be disdain.

After casting another glance at my spoiled cat, I grabbed the two plastic pitchers of tea I'd brewed the day before, tucked a sleeve of red cups under my arm, and headed back out just in time to meet Horatio and Isaiah in the driveway.

"Hi, guys," I said. "Want some tea?"

"Definitely, but first, we'll help you carry that." Isaiah took one pitcher and the cups before Horatio slipped the other pitcher from my hands.

Normally, I might have protested that I could carry something, but it was so hot and humid that I was glad to have my hands free to wipe the sweat off my forehead. "Thanks. What brings you by?"

"Just stopping in to be sure the crew made it," Horatio said. "We use these guys all the time, and they're really the best around. But we want to be sure everything is all set for this weekend."

"And next weekend!" Isaiah added. "Congratulations."

"Thanks," I said. "We hope you'll both come. I have an invitation for you inside, in fact."

"We'd be honored," Horatio said as we made it down to Sawyer's playground and set the cups and pitchers out for the workers.

Horatio poured himself, Isaiah, and me a glass and turned to me. "Any chance you guys have found out more information about Isaiah II?"

Isaiah VIII turned to me eagerly, and I took a deep breath as I tried to decide what to say. I didn't want to keep anything about his family from him, but the fact that his great-grandfather had accused two men of killing his father for money wasn't something to just share in casual conversation.

Fortunately, Santi saved me the trouble of deciding how to proceed when he walked over and said, "Gentlemen, we have some information we need to share. Feel like a little porch sit?"

My porch gave us a view of the work area, and the crewman that Sawyer had adopted seemed to have adopted him right back. So the four of us strolled back up the hill with our tea to take up seats on the porch. I turned on the porch fan, and by some miracle, the combination of the tea and the light breeze made the location rather pleasant.

Within five minutes, Santi had given Isaiah and Horatio the rundown on what Xzanthia had learned about the alleged murderers of Isaiah II. "Now, while that does sound like pretty damning information—"

Isaiah interrupted. "It's just hearsay." He nodded. "I get it." He took a sip of his tea as he looked down over the wildflowers below. "Plus, and I'm just spitballing here, doesn't it seem odd that Isaiah III would ask for help identifying the killers if he knew who they were all along?"

"Well, we don't know that he could identify them right away, do we?" I suggested.

Horatio nodded. "True, but if they killed his father for money, did they rob him at Mackey's place? Was Sylvester living there? If not, it seems kind of odd that he would end up there."

Santi had taken out his notebook and was jotting things down. "Do we know who was living here when LeVarge was murdered?"

"That's a good question," I said. "I assumed it was Joel Mackey, but I didn't compare the title records with the death date. One sec." I had all that information written down and went inside to get my notes.

"So we think your great-grandfather was killed on October 5, 1878, right?"

The three men nodded.

"Right," Isaiah said, "and I confirmed that with Mary from his death certificate. Cause of death was 'murder by stabbing,'" he said, using his fingers to make air quotes to show the actual wording on the certificate.

"So the property is owned by someone from out of state at that point, a Louis Hudson from New York. The title records indicate he bought it at auction, probably because Mackey couldn't afford the taxes and the State foreclosed." I shook my head. "But that means no one was living there at the time of the murder." I couldn't believe I hadn't put this together before.

"That would mean, then, that LeVarge was either there and

robbed before being killed, robbed before and brought there to be killed, or robbed and killed somewhere else before being brought there to be"—Santi looked at Isaiah—"sorry—disposed of."

Horatio rocked forward in his chair. "This whole situation keeps getting stranger. All this time, I'd thought the murder happened here because LeVarge lived here—do we know he definitely wasn't living here?"

"He could have been squatting here, I suppose, or maybe he was renting from the current owner." I took out my phone. "Just a second."

I jotted off a text to Xzanthia, hoping I wasn't waking her, copying in Mary, and asked if they had seen anything that said whether someone was living in my house in 1878. I told them the owner on record was from New York, but I wondered if someone could have been renting.

Xzanthia responded almost immediately. "Nothing I've seen, but since the Mackeys had sold by then, it probably wouldn't be noted in their papers."

I grimaced, but then Mary responded. "Yep, the LeVarges were living there until 1885 when they bought the land my daddy inherited."

I sucked in air. "Your family lived here, Isaiah," I said. "Mary must have records." My phone was going off with messages.

"Why?" Mary asked.

"Have you found something new?" Xzanthia wanted to know.

"I'll tell you more when you come for dinner at five p.m. We're having hot dogs."

"Can you guys stay for dinner?" I said.

11

The tent went up without difficulty, despite Sawyer's continued help, and as predicted, he proved himself scarily good at using a sledgehammer. I comforted myself with the fact that he'd always have work if he wanted it.

When he came in, and the truck with the tent crew left, we were all sweaty and tired, and Sawyer was ready to play video games. Fortunately, Isaiah was a big fan of Nintendo, so the two of them settled into the couch beside Beauregard, who quickly claimed Isaiah's lap. Horatio and Santi took a walk down to the stream to look at the trees the neighbors had planted and, I suspected, to talk a bit more about the case.

I took the opportunity to clean my kitchen up, prep a couple of bowls of chips, dig out the two liters of soda I kept hidden beside the washing machine, and then sat down and sewed for a few minutes while I listened to my new favorite podcast, *You're Wrong About*.

I'd finished a beautiful poppy in the past few days, and the next flower in the row of mason jars was a sunflower, Sawyer's favorite, and a brightly colored piece that was both easy to work and good for my spirit. I had almost finished two petals by the time I needed to put the hot dogs in the air fryer, and my spirits were certainly lifted.

At first, Sawyer claimed hot dogs were disgusting but ate two full ones and almost his weight in chips. We were all perched on the porch in various seats—Isaiah, Horatio, Xzanthia, Mary, Santi, Dad, Lucille, and I—while Sawyer kept us entertained with his antics, which involved leaping off the porch at full speed, chasing imaginary bears around the yard, also at full speed, and trying to coax Beauregard to "sing." Beau was not willing, of course, which made the whole performance even funnier.

Soon after we ate, Dad and Lucille took Sawyer for ice cream, and the rest of us got down to business. I quickly reviewed everything Xzanthia had found and that Mary had shared to ensure we were all up to speed. Then I sat down and let the conversation begin.

"My questions," Isaiah started, "all have to do with the things that don't make sense. Now I'm beginning to understand how Isaiah III might have seen his father being killed, and it makes sense that Isaiah II's body was here if he was killed here, of course, which would make sense if they lived here." Then he shook his head. "But why would Mackey and Robinson be here?"

"Maybe they knew your great-grandfather had money?" Santi suggested.

Xzanthia shook her head. "He could have had some, sure, but we're talking only eleven years after this man was freed from slavery. He couldn't have accumulated much, and if he had, trust me, he wasn't bragging about it."

"So, maybe he had something else they wanted?" I asked. "Or maybe something at the house here was valuable?" I looked around and tried to think what might have been of worth on a small farm like this. The Mackeys had been farmers but mostly at a subsistence level. Even as a mason, Joel Mackey wouldn't have made much money. I couldn't see there being a trove of valuables here, especially after the family moved away. "You're right, though. We're missing something," I finally said.

Mary looked at me and sighed. "Some mysteries can't be solved, I guess." She sounded so forlorn, and I could imagine why. Her ancestor had been murdered, and the people who killed him were never brought to justice. It seemed like no one had even noticed he was gone.

I sat up straighter. "That's it." I looked at Xzanthia, then Isaiah and Horatio, and finally Mary. "Did you see any other mentions that Isaiah II was killed or even missing? Anything in the public records or any of the family papers?"

Everyone sat for a minute, thinking and looking up at the blue ceiling of the porch or off into the field, but then every single person shook their head. "Nothing," Xzanthia said.

"No mention at all in our family stuff," Mary said. "And that's weird. That's what you're thinking, right, Pais?"

"Exactly. A man disappears, is just gone from the world as far as anyone knows, and the only mention of it is his son asking for help to find his murderer? Something else is going on here." Somewhere in the deepest part of my body, I could feel we were right.

Santi stood up. "Help me with how it might have been for a Black man during this time?" He looked at Xzanthia and then Mary. "Would anyone have contacted the police about his disappearance?"

Xzanthia shook her head. "Probably not. It wasn't likely the police would do anything, and it might even bring negative consequences for the family."

"What kind of consequences?" Horatio asked.

"Added scrutiny," Mary said. "Perhaps outright harassment. Jim Crow days were brutal."

Santi nodded. "Okay, so it's not odd that a formal police report wasn't filed. Got it. And I know what y'all have said about the community keeping some things quiet, secret even. But if everyone was worried that this man had been killed, and if his son was talking about it in public, even in a safe community like his church, don't we think we'd see evidence of it somewhere else?"

"Like church records?" Xzanthia said with a look at Mary. "You ever seen records from that church?"

"Nope, not a one, but that doesn't mean they're not out there." She took her plate and stood up. "I've got some phone calls to make. I'll see if we can't find where those records would be."

"If they survived the fire, that is," Xzanthia added as she rose beside Mary. "Off to recruit folks for Saturday. See you all later."

The rest of the group slowly made their way off, too, and soon, it was just me, Sawyer, Santi, Dad, and Lucille around a bonfire that Dad and Saw had made expressly for roasting marshmallows.

"So, just throwing this out," Lucille said as she double-stacked her marshmallows on her stick and put it over the fire. "Do we think that Isaiah III might have been lying?"

I glanced at Santi, who kept his gaze on the flames as his marshmallow turned into a charred brick. "That's what you're thinking, isn't it?" I said.

"I was trying to calm my intuition here," he said quietly. "I just kept telling myself that this was a historical situation and that history isn't my specialty." He looked up at me. "But yeah, I think there's a good chance that Isaiah LeVarge III lied."

"Yeah," I said. "So that's awkward."

"And implicating," Dad added.

Even Sawyer didn't have anything to say after that.

. . .

THE NEXT DAY, with Sawyer off at his dad's, was a whirlwind of activity that included checking in with Claire and Randy to ensure both of them were ready for the weekend since I was going to be completely wrapped up in genealogy day. Then The Pie Guy had questions about the setup that only I could answer, given that I was the only one who knew about the one external electrical outlet at the house. Plus, I really wanted the house to be completely clean, even though I didn't think anyone would be coming in. So I spent the afternoon with ear pods in and podcasts on as I made even my windows shine.

By the time Santi came home, and we made soup and grilled cheese for dinner, our new Friday night favorite, I was exhausted from the cleaning and all the managing I'd done that day.

"Any word from Xzanthia or Mary?" he asked as we sat down on the porch to eat.

"They both texted to say they had put out the word and hoped someone might come with information tomorrow. Nothing definite yet, though." If I were honest, our supposition about Isaiah III's lie weighed on me, too. I really didn't want to have to tell my new friend that his great-grandfather had lied about the murder of his own father. But more than that, I didn't want to think about the reasons that a young man might have lied. This situation was already heavy enough without those possibilities.

"Tomorrow is going to be a big day," he said.

"In so many ways," I said. "But let's forget about tomorrow and just enjoy our night."

"Agreed." He leaned over and kissed me softly before looking down at my bowl of tomato soup. "Is there actually any soup in there?"

"I prefer my soup to be like cheddar and cracker stew, thank you very much," I said as I lifted a chunky, cheesy spoonful out of the bowl.

"It's like you're eating two grilled cheese sandwiches, just one with a bit of tomato," he said.

"Exactly."

I WENT to bed early that night, aware that I would wake up early in anticipation of the day's activities. Early, however, wasn't meant to be four thirty a.m. Yet, when I heard a vehicle pull in at that time, I was up almost as fast as my fiancé. We'd both been involved in incidents where people came to my home, and while this situation with the body of Isaiah LeVarge seemed far less volatile than previous investigations, it was still nerve-racking enough to make us hyper-aware.

Santi put a hand out behind him as we crept down the stairs, but I wasn't about to wait while he walked in on who knows what. So in my T-shirt and boxer shorts, I crept along behind him as he stepped into the living room, then the kitchen, and finally stood looking at the large white truck in the driveway.

"Isn't that Horatio's truck?" I said as I peered over his shoulder.

"It is," he said. "Let's give it a minute and see what's happening."

I was inclined to walk out and ask what was up, but I knew Santi's instincts were better for this kind of thing. So I waited—well, waited and peed. Middle age was no time to be testing my bladder's endurance.

When I returned to the kitchen, Santi had moved into the small pantry on the far side of the room and was now standing and looking out the window there.

"What's going on?" I whispered.

Santi shook his head. "Horatio and Isaiah just walked by. Let's go," he said.

I thought we were getting ready to head outside, and I was

trying to remember where I'd put my rubber shoes since I
hated wet feet more than almost anything. Then I realized he
just meant, "Let's go to the windows at the back of the house."
No shoes were required.

The problem was that the windows at the back of the house
didn't give us a line of sight to the actual back of the house.
That view was blocked by the creamery, so we couldn't see
anything more from there.

"Come with me," Santi whispered as he headed back
through the first floor and upstairs. Then he quietly lifted the
window in our bedroom and gestured for me to go out onto the
roof. I stared at him for a long minute, trying to decide if he
actually thought I was going to do this. "You want to see what's
going on or not?" he said quietly.

That was, of course, a ridiculous question. I always wanted
to know what was going on, so I swung my leg over the window
sill and stepped out onto the roof, where I immediately
crouched as low as I could.

"Did they see you?" Santi whispered as he joined me.

"What?" I looked down at myself. "Oh, no. I just feel safer
closer to the shingles."

Santi smiled. "Come on, woman." He turned around and
made his way down the slope at the back of the house, then put
one foot on the breezeway roof to test it. "It'll hold," he said.

"It'll hold" is not exactly the shining assurance of structural
integrity that a woman who is terrified of heights hopes to hear
when she's about to creep across a roof to spy on people she
really likes who might be doing something terribly nefarious in
her backyard.

Still, I followed my fiancé across the very old metal roof,
trying to be quiet while also trying to keep myself from sliding
off the roof. It was not easy.

We made it across the small building, though, and from the
edge, we could see across the backyard and all the way down to

the tent. It took me a bit, but eventually, I discerned the figures of two men lying prone beside my office. It looked like they had long sticks or something and were poking them under the building.

I looked at Santi but didn't dare say anything because I would have easily been heard.

He shrugged, and both of us turned back to watch the men in action . . . and that was when my satin boxers betrayed me, sending me sliding down the side of the roof and right onto the grass with an *oomph*.

The next few moments were like a skit from the Three Stooges. I landed on the ground and groaned. Isaiah startled and banged his head on the bottom of my office while Horatio stood up and started wielding a broom toward the sky, where Santi sat looking quite like a gargoyle against the half-moon.

IT TOOK A FEW MINUTES, but we eventually all calmed down enough to talk through what was going on. "What are you doing here?" I asked after Santi had brought me a large ice pack and helped me settle into a lumpy, cold seat on the couch with a cup of coffee.

"We are so sorry," Isaiah said as he and Horatio sat down across the room with their own mugs of coffee.

Santi sat as close to me as Beauregard would allow, given Beau's strange desire to be a great caretaker of his people, but only when they were injured. "What was going on back there?"

The two men quickly came running to help me when they realized I was the source of the loud thump and consequent groaning. When Santi jumped down from the low end of the creamery a moment later, Horatio had bravely turned to wield his broom sword at the intruder, only to start uncontrollably laughing when he realized it was Santi.

"Oh goodness, you scared us," Horatio had said as he dropped his broom.

"We scared you?" I'd said as they helped me to my feet. "Wait, before you explain, I need coffee . . . and ibuprofen."

Now, here we were, iced, medicated, and caffeinated, and I needed a lot more information. "This will be a great story one day, I expect, but really, what are you doing here?" I said again as the caffeine hit my bloodstream and my synapses started to fire at a normal speed.

"We thought we could get here, complete our project, and get out before you woke up. Were we that loud?" Horatio said.

"Well, your truck isn't exactly stealthy," Santi said. "But we're also both a little keyed up."

I was starting to get impatient and cleared my throat. "Seriously, what are you doing here?" I may or may not have screeched a little.

"Oh, sorry," Isaiah said. "We wanted to clean up under the office—you know, get the few remnants of old trash out and then tack up some lattice before planting a few flowers. I just wanted to do something for my great-grandfather and you, but I knew you two would probably want to help if we tried during daylight hours."

"You were going to put up lattice work in the middle of the night without us hearing you?" Santi said with a slow smile spreading across his face. "Do you have a silencer for your hammers?"

Horatio blushed. "A pneumatic nail gun with paneling nails. I guess it wouldn't have been as quiet as I thought." He glanced toward the back window. "And I had forgotten the chickens are right next door."

I started to laugh. "Oh, the girls would have raised a ruckus for sure. And Xavier would have been crowing to high heaven." My laughter sank to my stomach, and soon, I was cackling so hard that my coffee threatened to spill.

Santi took my mug from me and gently patted my knee. "You all right there?" he asked.

I nodded, unable to speak because of the image of the nail gun waking the chickens who, in turn, would have definitely woken us ... that is, if the nail gun hadn't done so already.

"You're lucky I didn't draw my gun," Santi said while I continued to chuckle.

Isaiah's eyes went wide. "I didn't even think of that," he said.

That sent me into even harder laughter, and the harder I laughed, the more my bruised bottom hurt. And as I remembered my slide off the room and the ensuing mayhem, I laughed more. Soon, tears rolled down my cheeks, and the three men looked at me like I might need some oxygen or a sedative.

I finally calmed down, though, and the four of us sat for a bit, just sipping coffee and gathering our thoughts. At least, that was what I was doing because I knew, in the way we sometimes just know things, that this was the time I needed to tell Isaiah our suspicions about Isaiah III's lie at the old church.

"I actually love what you're doing, and we'll finish it up as soon as the sun comes up," I said. "Unless, of course, you prefer working in the dark," I added with a wink."

"Sunrise is fine," Isaiah said. "Thanks for not being mad."

Santi shook his head. "Tonight, when we're so tired we can hardly see, we plan on coming over for dinner," he quipped.

"Absolutely. Steak, potatoes, and grilled asparagus, okay?" Horatio asked, and he wasn't kidding.

"Are you kidding?" I asked. When he shook his head, I said, "That sounds amazing! Thanks."

Isaiah smiled. "Of course, but while we're waiting for the sun, I need to ask you something." His face grew serious. "Do you think Isaiah III was lying when he said two men killed his dad?"

I looked at Santi, whose face had gone very still, and then

turned back to Isaiah. "Yes," I said. "Why do you ask?" I had so much I wanted to say, but context mattered, especially when it came to talking about family.

"It's just the only thing that makes sense," Horatio said. "We've been talking about it for a couple of days now, and honestly, if you take away what Isaiah III said, there's no reason to suspect anyone else."

I nodded and thought about that statement for a minute. I had been concentrating on what the teenage boy said at church, but now I realized we suspected Mackey and Robinson because of what Isaiah II said later in life, too. "You're right," I said. "But he was murdered. That's scientific fact."

"He was," Isaiah said. "But when someone goes so hard to point the finger at someone else for something . . ." He looked over at Santi.

"They probably had reason to get people looking another direction," Santi said. "I'm with you. I think Isaiah III probably killed his father."

Even though we had all walked into this conversation with the same possible theory, the moment still felt heavy and awkward. We suspected Isaiah's great-grandfather of not only being a murderer but of committing patricide. This was no small supposition.

"Tell me why you think that?" I finally asked.

Isaiah nodded. "It's the only thing that makes sense of his lies. If he hadn't killed his father, why say anything at all? Why not just let him go missing?"

"Right," Horatio added. "Or say he's missing?"

"But if you say he's missing," Santi said, "then people might go looking for him, and if they did, they might find him." He was nodding.

I sipped my coffee as I let the knot of confusion in my mind unwind. "But wouldn't people have gone looking for his body if his son said he had been killed? At least to bury him?"

"That's where I'm stuck, too," Isaiah said. "Maybe today, we'll find out they did go looking for his body." He didn't sound too convinced.

"Maybe," I said. "And forgive me for suggesting this, but what if everyone knew that Isaiah III had killed him but quietly decided just to let the murder go? A sort of collective silence or something?"

Isaiah shrugged. "Could be. I'm just so puzzled by everything here . . . but mostly why my great-grandfather would kill his father."

"Let's hope we find out today," Santi said as he stood up. "Now, what do you say we finish up what these men started?"

I slowly stood and said, "As long as I can do anything I need to do prone, I'm good." My tuchus hurt something fierce. I expected it was going to be a while before I could sit comfortably.

"You, then, are in charge of sweeping under the office," Horatio said as we walked out the back door. He handed me his broom.

"I feel like maybe you should knight me with this or something. You had some great moves with it." I laughed as I took it from his hand. "Show me your ways."

The man rolled his eyes at me and then helped me lie down on my belly with my head and shoulders under the office. "So what am I doing?"

Isaiah lay down across from me and said, "It doesn't make much sense, I know, but I just wanted to make the dirt look nice." He smiled, but his face still looked sad.

"I completely understand," I said and began moving the broom back and forth to level the dirt and, perhaps, remove any remaining debris from under the building. We'd taken a lot of the trash out when we'd cleaned up around the body, but in the other areas under the building, I could still see the rims of bottles and a couple of pieces of what looked like blue plastic.

The two of us worked to push everything out from under the building and then simply swept the dirt thoroughly before sliding out and standing up. Meanwhile, Horatio and Santi had cut the lattice to the right sizes and started to bag up the remaining trash we'd removed.

I walked over to be sure there weren't any valuable bottles or things in the debris as Santi dropped each piece into the garbage bag, and that was when I saw it—a silver ring with a small blue stone.

I lunged toward the ground and grabbed it. "What in the world?" I said.

Isaiah leaned forward and studied the piece of jewelry. "I've seen that ring before," he said. "It was Isaiah III's."

12

The four of us went back inside, cleaned off the ring, and sat down at the dining room table with it in the center. "Where did you see him wearing this?" I asked Isaiah. "Was it in the newspaper picture?" I tried to remember the image of the tall thin man with the mustache and his prize pumpkin, but I didn't recall seeing a ring, but since I hadn't been looking for jewelry in the photo, that wasn't surprising.

"I didn't see him wearing it," he said. "My dad wears it on a chain he keeps around his neck. He has always told me it would be mine one day, that it had been passed down for five generations."

"But if he wears it on a chain around his neck . . ." Santi didn't have to finish his thought.

"Exactly. I don't know," Isaiah said. "But this ring is exactly the same as my dad's."

"So there are two?" Horatio said as he carefully picked up the ring and looked it over. "Why would someone have two identical rings made?"

"Best friends? Mother and daughter?" I suggested, but then

I looked at the ring's size. It was too big for the fingers of most of the women I knew. "Or maybe—"

"Husbands," Isaiah and Horatio said at the same time.

The rightness of that lit a bit of knowledge in the center of my chest. "Isaiah II was gay?"

"Or Isaiah III. Maybe he lost his ring when he put his father under the office?" Horatio suggested.

Santi shook his head. "But both of these men had children, so they couldn't have been . . ."

My withering look stopped him short. "You know better than that, Santiago Shifflett," I said. "Gay people have children all the time."

"And in that time period, most gay men had a woman close by, sometimes even as their wife, to keep them from being found out," Horatio said. "It just wasn't safe."

I nodded. "That makes sense. And if you were married and didn't have children but spent time with a certain man, then people would talk. So you did what you needed to do."

"Exactly," Isaiah said. "Plus, it takes some people a long time to figure out they're gay. Haven't you seen the #lateinlife-lesbian tag on TikTok?"

"I'm not on TikTok," Santi said, "but I hear you. Forgive me. Sometimes the way I was raised still rises up."

Horatio shook his head. "No worries. We're all learning all the time." He looked down at the ring again. "But I really am confused by this ring. Who was Isaiah III married to?"

Isaiah shook his head. "I have no idea, but I'd sure like to find out."

"The good news is that we have a ton of people coming here in"—I looked up at the clock on the stove—"a couple of hours who might be able to shed some light on this particular mystery."

"And we'd better get cracking," Santi said.

Within a few minutes, all three men were busy getting

extension cords, directing the truck with the porta potties, and planting the extra flowers in front of the house. I, at their insistence, was back on my ice pack seat and sewing. Aside from my sore rear, I didn't mind that at all because I was going to get my fill of people and questions soon enough.

PLUS, I wanted to ponder what we'd discovered that morning. Something was niggling at me, and I needed some time alone to figure it out. So we knew that Isaiah III had been wearing a ring identical to the one we'd found under the office in that 1926 picture, a fact I had confirmed with Xzanthia that morning, and presumably, that ring was the one that had been passed down to our Isaiah's father.

But the question that finally settled out from the spinning information in my mind was whether or not the ring had belonged to Isaiah II first. Could he have been wearing the ring when he was killed, and that was why it was under there? Or had the ring been Isaiah III's, and he'd lost it—as his great-grandson suggested—when he hid the body? And if so, then how had Isaiah III come to get the matching ring?

I felt like I needed a chart to keep track of who was who and with who, and I once again wished that, despite the significance of passing down a name, people had been inclined to bequeath original names to each generation. After all, we could still find out that Isaiah's son was named Caspian, and it would be a whole lot easier to keep them straight in research.

Soon enough, though, my stitching and pondering time was over, and I put my needle on my bear needle holder and surveyed the sunflower I'd just finished. It looked lovely, and I felt restored a bit, even if my rear was still achy.

. . .

THE PEOPLE BEGAN to arrive right at ten, and I was glad Saul and
Dad had thought through a parking plan and had brought
volunteers to direct folks to park beside the garden, where the
ground was firm enough not to require the use of winches or
tow straps later in the day.

Horatio and Isaiah had gone out and put up signs on the road
to guide people in, and Mika and Lucille had set up a drink station
—complete with sodas, coolers of ice, and copious amounts of
sweet tea—next to The Pie Guy's truck. The porta potties were
placed on the far side of the house and down in the field under the
tent. Xzanthia and Mary were ready with the scanners and their
computers to answer questions, take notes, and help people digi-
tize their photos for the new website Isaiah had built.

I was too sore to do much more than sit in a chair and direct
people in the right direction when they arrived, but that turned
out okay since it meant I got to say hello and introduce myself
to everyone. I'd grown up in Octonia, but that didn't mean I
knew everybody, especially when it came to the Black community. We were making strides at integration still, but the legacy
of slavery and Jim Crow still kept a lot of us apart.

At one point, when five little boys were chasing each other
through the yard as they played tag and shrieked, I missed
Sawyer and wished he was there. But then I moved and realized
that the last thing I needed right now was an energetic
preschooler who might just end up on the roof himself.

Once the arrivals started to slow, I made my way down to
the tent and took up a post at one of the scanners. I scanned
images of women in their wedding gowns and photos of folks
on their front porches, not one of them smiling as was the
fashion of the time. I scanned four-by-four snapshots that
looked like they could have come from my childhood, and I
even managed to get clear images of a few Polaroids.

When I looked over at Xzanthia, she was fairly glowing as

she answered genealogical questions, made notes about further queries, and encouraged people to stop by and visit the historical society for more information. The stack of brochures and envelopes about memberships to the society was noticeably smaller by midafternoon, and I hoped that meant she'd get some more members.

The crowd was so robust that we barely had any time to talk to one another, and the men were kept busy with traffic duty, questions about the property, and not a small number of requests to see the place where Isaiah II's body had been found. My newsletter article had gotten the word out, and people were curious.

Some folks were family, Isaiah's and Mary's cousins, but others were just looky-loos, the sort who ogled at car crashes on the highway. But Isaiah was gracious with everyone.

At three forty-five, a hearse pulled into the driveway. As planned, we shut down the computers and encouraged anyone interested to join us at the back of the property for a brief memorial service in honor of Isaiah II. Saul's crew had dug the hole earlier in the morning, and the local funeral home donated their car and tents for the service.

Precisely at four, Isaiah, Horatio, Santi, Saul, and Mary's nephew carried the coffin to the gravesite and set it on the casket lowering system, as I'd learned it was called earlier in the day when the funeral home's crew came to set it up. Then, as the casket lowered into the ground, the men stood silently by and watched it.

At that point, our pastor said a few words about the importance of family and legacy, about memories and histories. He didn't even try to speak about the deceased since it would have been patently untruthful given the situation here, but he did talk about the family, about how they were caring and kind and that, in his experience, that kind of demeanor came from generations of teaching about love and compassion. It was a lovely, appropriate message.

When he was done, Isaiah VIII stepped forward and tossed a shovel full of dirt onto the casket. Horatio followed suit, and slowly, the almost one hundred people in attendance did the same, paying tribute to a man who had died almost a hundred and fifty years ago. It was a beautiful moment, and when the crowd began to disperse after singing "Amazing Grace," I had tears in my eyes.

"That was beautiful," I said to Isaiah as we headed back to the tent to gather the equipment.

"It was. Thank you for giving him this place to rest," he said.

"You're most welcome. This was his home, and again, you are welcome to visit here anytime." I smiled. "Okay, maybe not at four a.m., but any other time."

Santi joined us. "We also wanted you to know that we've filed the site of the cemetery with the Department of Historic Resources so that it will be protected in the future. This is now officially a LeVarge family cemetery, and if anyone else in your family wishes to be buried here, the space will be here for you." He pointed to where Saul was inserting stakes in the twenty-by-twenty-foot space that Santi and I had decided we'd preserve.

"Feel no pressure," I added. "We know you have other family members buried elsewhere. But this space is here should you or your family ever want it." I met Isaiah's gaze, and my tears mirrored his.

He hugged me and said, "You have no idea how much that means. Thank you."

Horatio joined us and said, "Are we all ready for steaks?"

I nodded. "But first, more ibuprofen."

IT TURNED out that Horatio and Isaiah had invited everyone for not just steak but ribeye steak, so Dad, Lucille, Santi, and I rode over together and met Xzanthia, Mary, and Mika there. Even Saul decided to join us, bringing a couple of cases of locally brewed beer with him. We were clearly celebrating.

The thing was, I wasn't sure what we were celebrating. After all, we'd just buried a man today, a man who had been murdered. But then, we'd had a hundred and fifty-seven people turn out for an event we'd announced just a week ago, and I was dying to hear what Xzanthia and Mary had learned during the day.

But first, we needed to eat. And eat we did. The meal was scrumptious, and I demanded Horatio's recipe for the grilled asparagus. It was almost better than the steak. Almost.

After we finished the meal, we gathered on their back porch with beers, ciders, and glasses of wine to sit around their gas-fired, blue-flamed firepit that looked like it had come out of a very trendy Northern Virginia pub. We heard how they came to live on this piece of land, about twenty acres at the edge of a town called Somerset, how they'd found the land and built their dream house three years ago and planned to live here until the day they died.

"And this time next year, a little girl will be here with us."

"What?" I shouted. "You're having a baby?"

"Avery Grace," Horatio said. "She's due in March."

Of course, the conversation wove around little Avery for a long time after that, and I was on my second beer when Isaiah steered the conversation back to the day's events. "So it was a great day, and I'm so grateful we were able to bury Isaiah II properly." He sighed. "But I still don't feel like we're done."

Mika agreed. "I know, and we spent the whole day answering questions. I just hope maybe we got some answers, too. Did we?" She looked from Xzanthia to Mary.

Mary smiled and looked over at Xzanthia, who nodded. "We did," Mary said.

I stared at my friends, sure they had a sort of information

presentation they were about to give, and sure enough, Xzanthia took her laptop out of her bag. "Maybe you can all stand
behind me to see?"

Within seconds, we gathered behind Xzanthia and her
computer, and she began what was clearly a full-on slide show.
"This, Isaiah, as you know, is your father, Isaiah VII. For future
reference, please notice the necklace on his neck." She had a
picture on the screen of a man who looked remarkably like our
Isaiah but with a shorter fade and two earrings in his right ear.

"And this is your grandfather, Isaiah VI." The photo looked
like it came from 1950, and the man in it was leaning against a
very red, finned car that Santi probably knew the name of.

"Here is Isaiah V at his wedding to your great-grandmother,
Ida, and this is Isaiah IV. He was also a stone mason and helped
build the high school here in Octonia," she continued.

I looked over at Isaiah, and his eyes were wide. Horatio had
his arm around his waist and pulled him close.

"We've all seen this picture before." She showed the newspaper photo of Isaiah III and his prize pumpkin. "This time,
please note the ring on his left pinky finger." Sure enough,
there was the exact ring we'd found just that morning under
my office.

Isaiah pulled the ring we'd found out of his pocket. "It's
exactly the same," he said as Xzanthia zoomed in on Isaiah III's
left hand.

"It is," she said, "and when I spoke with your dad about it
this afternoon, he said that the stone was just glass but that
your grandfather had always told everyone it was a star
sapphire."

"You talked to my dad?" Isaiah asked. "Today?"

"I arranged a little meet and greet while you were busy
preparing for the service," Santi said with a wink at Horatio.

"That's how you guys were able to pull this all together," I
said with a laugh. "You're sneaky."

"Sneaky and thorough," Xzanthia said. "Here, we have the only known photo of Isaiah II, taken in 1877 as part of a photographic essay about the construction of the courthouse here." The picture showed a group of workers, each posed with their hand on a stone on a low wall. Above each person was their last name. The third man from the left was labeled, LeVarge.

Isaiah gasped. "That's him," he said in a hushed voice. "Wow."

I stared at the photo and tried to get a closer look at the man's hand. Xzanthia glanced over her shoulder at me.

"Does this help?" she said as she clicked over to a grainy image of what was, apparently, Isaiah LeVarge's left hand.

There, fuzzy but still discernible, was a ring with a single round stone in the center. "Amazing," Lucille whispered.

"He's wearing the ring," Isaiah said. "It was his."

"It was," Mary said as Xzanthia stood up and handed her the computer. "It took some real digging, but we figured out that your eight-times great-grandfather, Isaiah, was married to a man named Jonah Washington." She clicked to a photo of a White man in a long frock coat holding a cane. "This is Jonah."

It seemed like everyone held their breath for a moment, then finally, Dad said, "He's White."

That statement's obviousness broke the moment's spell, and Isaiah started to laugh. "Yes, yes, he is," he said between chuckles.

"That's amazing," Mika said. "How did you find out who his husband was?"

Mary grinned. "That's an interesting story." She set the laptop aside, and everyone took their seats. "Today, a woman came up to me and said she'd heard that Isaiah LeVarge was found on this land. She asked me if I knew he'd been murdered."

From there, Mary told us that the woman had been the granddaughter of the last pastor of the "old church," and the family had passed down a story about Isaiah II and his murder. The story was that Isaiah had been very sick, probably with cancer, and he'd been in a great deal of pain at the end of his life.

"Apparently," Mary continued, "everyone around Isaiah II knew he was gay and that he and Jonah were, if not legally, in every other way married. But they also knew if the wider Octonia community knew that, Isaiah and Jonah would suffer, maybe even be killed."

I shook my head. It was ridiculous, and sadly, some people still felt like people shouldn't be able to love who they loved.

"So when it became clear that LeVarge was dying," Mary said, "the family, including Isaiah's legal wife, invited Jonah over, and the two men were able to be together until almost the end."

This wasn't going to end well, I knew it, so I grabbed Santi's hand for support.

"But someone must have talked about what was going on because, in Isaiah's last hours, a family friend came running and told them that the police were on their way to arrest the two men for indecency," Mary said quietly.

Uncle Saul swore, and it was a fitting reaction.

"So rather than let his father die in jail or let the love of his father's life be arrested, Isaiah III"—Mary took a deep breath—"looked at his father, who gave him a single nod, then stabbed him three times before quickly hiding his body under the kitchen behind the house."

I gasped and squeezed Santi's hand as tightly as I could. "He was fourteen," I said.

"Just a baby," Xzanthia said.

"But also a brave, brave man," Dad added. "That took courage."

Isaiah looked at Horatio. "He did that for us, love."

A tear slid down Horatio's cheek. "I'll forever be grateful," he said before leaning over and kissing his husband. "I love you," he whispered.

It took a while to absorb that news, and we sat quietly for quite a long time. I thought about how even my own engagement wouldn't have been legal until just a few decades before, and it had only been a few years back that Isaiah and Horatio were allowed to marry. Human beings and the systems we create could be profoundly awful to other humans. It was heartbreaking in every way.

Eventually, though, hope does shine through, and Xzanthia picked up the thread of hope at the same time she picked up her second glass of wine. "The story doesn't end completely bleakly, though. Jonah Washington became a very well-to-do businessman in Washington, D.C., and according to the woman Mary and I met today, he continued to care for Isaiah's legal family as if they were his own because, of course, they were."

"He sent Isaiah III and his siblings to college at Howard, and they all lived with their second dad, as they came to call Jonah when they had distance from Octonia. Eventually, when Isaiah's legal wife needed nursing care, Jonah paid for a young woman to live with and care for her in her own home on land he had helped to finance once Isaiah III was older and decided to return to Octonia."

"But, by then, your house, Paisley, had been sold to someone else, and there wasn't any way for him to come back and properly bury his father. So his father's body lay there until, well, until you found it," Mary finished.

I slowly shook my head. "I cannot believe it." I sighed and swallowed back my tears. "What a privilege to have a small part in this incredible story."

"Indeed," Xzanthia said as she raised her glass. "To Isaiah

and Jonah, and to the community of the old church who protected them all these years."

We toasted to their memory and began gathering our things to return to our homes. I wanted to get to mine and sit by Isaiah II's grave for a bit.

But just as we were about to leave, Isaiah said, "Wait, who was the woman who told you all this?" He looked expectantly at Mary and Xzanthia.

"Oh, that's maybe the best part," Mary said. "She's Jonah Washington's four-times great-granddaughter, Isa Washington." Mary handed Isaiah a piece of paper. "When you're ready, she'd very much like to meet her cousin and the man who carries the name of the man she is named for."

IN TIME, we came to learn that Jonah Washington had married a woman in D.C., a woman he respected, admired, and loved in a very real way but who was also aware he was a gay man. She'd happily offered him a kind of protection, even as he gave her a level of security that wasn't available to many women at that time. They had one son, who they called Jonah after his father, but his middle name was Isaiah.

Mary later told me for the newsletter article I wrote the following week that Jonah Isaiah Washington was a name passed down through four generations. But when the fifth-generation couple had a girl, they named her Isa, wanting the name to continue. It was this woman who called the historical society to inquire about the story after reading my first newsletter article.

The rest, as they say, was history. Hard, happy, history, as it all is.

EPILOGUE

A week later, in a casual ceremony just up the hill from the grave of Isaiah LeVarge, Santiago Shifflett and I were married. We wrote our own vows. He promised to keep me in cross-stitch supplies, and I vowed to do my best to stay out of his police investigations. Sawyer carried our rings and did a spectacular forward flip, with the rings still in his pocket, up the center aisle. I'm fairly sure he received more applause than we did.

I carried a bouquet of sunflowers, zinnias, calendula, and marigolds that I had grown myself, and Santi had a simple marigold boutonniere. I wore a simple linen sheath and a pair of the most comfortable sandals I'd ever had, gold and sparkly Chacos that Mika somehow found for the special day.

Dad and Lucille gave me away, and Santi's mother cheered when he said, "I do." I guess she felt it was about time. And when we walked back down the aisle to "American Woman" by Lenny Kravitz, our friends streamed out of the folding chairs to dance behind us all the way to the tent.

The reception went well into the wee hours of the morning, as all good receptions should, and Sawyer and Beauregard curled up under the cake table and fell asleep together. The photographer had a heyday with that opportunity.

The day was absolutely perfect in every way, especially since when we finally went to bed—all three of us together because, well, that was what our family looked like at that moment—Santi said, "Oh, love, it feels so good to finally be home."

A FREE COZY SET IN SAN FRANCISCO

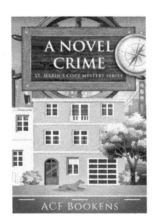

Join my Cozy Up email group for weekly book recommendations & a FREE copy of *A Novel Crime*, the prequel to my St. Marin's Cozy Mystery Series.
Sign up here - https://bookens.andilit.com/CozyUp

ALSO BY ACF BOOKENS

St. Marin's Cozy Mystery Series

Publishable By Death

Entitled To Kill

Bound To Execute

Plotted For Murder

Tome To Tomb

Scripted To Slay

Proof Of Death

Epilogue of An Epitaph

Hardcover Homicide

Picture Book Peril

Dog-Eared Danger - Coming June 2023

Stitches In Crime Series

Crossed By Death

Bobbins and Bodies

Hanged By A Thread

Counted Corpse

Stitch X For Murder

Sewn At The Crime

Blood And Backstitches

Fatal Floss

Strangled Skein

Aida Time

Poe Baxter Books Series

Fatalities And Folios

Massacre And Margins

Butchery And Bindings

Monograph and Murder - Coming in February 2023

Spines and Slaughter - Coming in March 2023

ABOUT THE AUTHOR

ACF Bookens lives in Virginia's Southwestern Mountains with her young son, an old hound, and a bully mix who has already eaten two couches. When she's not writing, she cross-stitches, watches YA fantasy shows, and grows massive quantities of cucumbers. Find her at acfbookens.com.

Printed in the USA
CPSIA information can be obtained
at www.ICGtesting.com
CBHW070544031224
18348CB00045B/540